MAGGIE

NETTA NEWBOUND

W0006624

Junction Publishing

United Kingdom - New Zealand

Junctionpublishing@outlook.com

www.junction-publishing.com

Publisher's Note: This is a work of fiction. Names, characters, places, and incidents are a product of the author's imagination. Locales and public names are sometimes used for atmospheric purposes. Any resemblance to actual people, living or dead, or to businesses, companies, events, institutions, or locales is completely coincidental.

Ordering Information:

Quantity sales. Special discounts are available on quantity purchases by corporations, associations, and others. For details, contact the "Special Sales Department" at the email address above.

Maggie/Netta Newbound -- 2nd ed.

I would like to dedicate this book to two wonderful women — my gorgeous mum, Lynda, and my amazing mother-in-law, Nova. Your continued support inspires me.

CHAPTER 1

The sounds of *Jerusalem*, my mother's favourite hymn, reverberated off the four walls of the quaint village chapel.

I couldn't sing. I could barely perform the most basic of functions as I stared at the casket that held her fragile and wasted body.

Breast cancer had been responsible for taking the best mother a girl could wish for. She'd found it too late, and the specialists had told her no amount of treatment would make any difference. So she'd made the call not to even try.

I couldn't believe how brave she'd been. And now, just four months after finding that first bastard lump, she was gone.

I'd helped to look after her as much as I could, but towards the end, the palliative care team took over. Then, last week, even the night times had been covered by a *Marie Curie* nurse. But still, I insisted on helping.

Mum seemed to be aware, and I could tell, by the look in her eyes, she was grateful.

My stepdad, Kenny, wasn't much help. In fact, he'd been a total waste of space. It seemed as though he thought if he ignored what was happening, then it wouldn't actually be true. He made me sick. They'd been married since I was eight, half my life, yet they'd never had any more children. I got the impression it had been his decision, not hers. Mum had enough love for a houseful of kids, but not him.

I glanced at him, standing beside me crying, his mouth wide as he bawled unashamedly. For a handsome man, he was certainly an ugly crier. But I envied his tears. I hadn't shed any since my mum took her final, rasping breath.

Kenny, or Kenneth Edmond Simms as he was known professionally, was the village accountant. He was well liked and looked up to by everyone he had any dealings with. But I'd noticed the way some of the local women had been looking at him when news of my mother's terminal illness had been made public.

I figured it wouldn't be long before he was parading his fancy women on his arm, without a thought for my poor mum. Even though I wasn't seventeen yet, I wasn't behind the door when it came to the psychology of men. As long as their meals were being made, their laundry done and their egos stroked, they were almost anybody's.

"You okay, Maggie?" Claudia, our next-door neighbour asked.

I nodded, suddenly back in the room, and I realised everybody was up on their feet as heavy gold curtains closed around the casket. Panic gripped me and my body shuddered.

As the congregation headed to the door, I turned and allowed myself to be caught up in the crowd. For that brief moment I was anonymous. Nobody looked at me with pity and sadness. But, when outside, the crowd dispersed and I was left feeling utterly alone and vulnerable.

"Maggie? Maggie!"

I turned, disorientated, and I couldn't tell where the voice was coming from. Then Claudia stepped from the sea of people and pulled me into her arms.

"Oh, my poor darling. Come, let me find you a seat – you look done in."

She ferried me back towards the doors just as Kenny emerged surrounded by well-wishers, mostly female.

Claudia barged amongst them. "Your daughter needs some attention, Kenneth. She's not looking too good. Maybe it's her asthma."

Kenny made a display of pulling me into his arms and sobbing. His tears soaked into my plain, grey dress. I didn't like dresses, but I'd decided I needed to make an effort for Mum.

Lots of comments and murmurs followed.

"Aw, how sweet. They will need each other now..."

"Emily was their rock..."

"So, so sad..."

I shut my ears to them – what the hell did they know? It was always the same; people saw one thing and would make their minds up about something they knew nothing about.

"Is everything set up at the house?" Kenny asked when we were alone in the back of the funeral car.

I nodded. The neighbours had all pulled together, led by Claudia, and helped prepare a buffet fit for a queen's send off.

"We'll get through it, you know. At least she's not suffering anymore. I couldn't bear seeing her like that."

I wanted to remind him he'd not seen much of her suffering anyway. He'd hardly been by her side during the final stages. But I didn't reply. My mother had taught me if I couldn't say anything nice, to keep my mouth shut.

Back at our modest home, I was surprised by how many people had actually followed us. I didn't think we'd get them all inside let alone feed them. But it didn't matter. They were there to pay their respects to my beautiful and funny mother. Nobody would care if they couldn't find a seat.

The sound of their voices clamouring together in our dinky, middle of the row, terraced house, made my head throb.

After a few minutes, I slid away to the comfort of my room and curled up on the bed.

But Kenny soon clicked I wasn't around, and came bursting in, demanding I make an appearance. I had a job to do and people needed looking after.

Reluctantly, I followed him back downstairs.

When everybody had gone, Kenny brought in several glasses from the front doorstep and placed them on the kitchen worktop.

"That was a decent send off," he said, with a smile.

I nodded, and continued loading the dishwasher.

"Look, Mags. You and I are all that's left. We need to support each other."

"I know." My words were no more than a whisper.

"We've never been very close, probably down to me, but I'm willing to make an effort, if you are?"

I shrugged and turned my back on him.

When I went through to the lounge later, I found him lying on the sofa.

"Go and get in bed, Mags. It's been a long day."

I noticed how pale and tired he looked and realised that maybe he *was* missing Mum after all. "Can I get you anything before I go up?"

"I couldn't face another thing, but thanks anyway." He smiled sadly. "I'll probably get an early night myself."

I heard him trudge up the stairs while I was in the bathroom. His bedroom door was already closed when I came out.

Mum had been sleeping in the front room, and so he was used to having the bed to himself.

The past few days, since Mum died, I'd felt out of place. Without her, where did I belong? Mum didn't have any family, I was her only living relative, and she mine – unless you counted my birth father who'd run out on us when I was barely six months old.

Without Mum, Kenny wouldn't want me hanging about, cramping his style.

I could get a job. I was old enough to legally leave school, although I had planned to stay on for sixth form and then, the following year, go to college to take my A levels. But, if need be, I could leave now.

We lived in a village called Harley on the outskirts of Manchester, and at a push, I could travel into the city by bus. But if I left school there would be no reason to stay in the village. I would just look for a bedsit close to wherever the job was.

It was thoughts of my future that had got me through the rest of the afternoon. Mum would have been mortified if she'd known my plans, since she'd had big dreams for me, but as far as I could see I had no choice.

In my room, I curled up on the bed and checked my phone, not really expecting any messages. Then I stalked a couple of the popular girls from school to see how their day had been. This was the extent of my social media activity. However, stalking wasn't really social at all.

The few friends I did have had stopped bothering with me when Mum had become sick. I was clearly no longer any fun. Mum always told me you soon discover who your true friends are in a crisis, and she was right.

Although summer, it was unusually hot for July in the north of England and the duvet I usually had was in the airing cupboard. I stripped off my clothes and slid between the cool sheets. So that was that. The day we buried my mother had been and gone and I still hadn't shed one tear.

I couldn't believe it had really happened. It was like some kind of awful nightmare that I couldn't wake up from.

Restless, I decided to go back downstairs and empty the dishwasher. I pulled on my lime-green satin pyjamas and padded down on bare feet.

Bending over the dishwasher, I didn't hear Kenny enter the kitchen. I almost had a heart attack when I stood up and saw him beside the sink filling a glass with water. I squealed and clutched my chest.

"Sorry," he said. "Couldn't you sleep either?"

I shook my head.

He sat at the kitchen table sipping his water.

When all the dishes were put away, I went back up to my room and lay on top of the sheets.

The silence of the house freaked me out, being used to the nurses coming and going, and Mum's random, fretful cries. Now there was just the two of us, Kenny and I, politely sidestepping each other – creeping about as though trying to avoid waking the dead.

I flicked through Facebook again. Rachel Mendoza, my ex-best friend, had posted several photos from her holiday in Ibiza, off the coast of Spain. That hurt. Surely she could have waited to post images of her and her family smiling happily for the camera. Didn't she know how heartless that was? Today of all days.

At last, silent tears ran down my cheeks as I flicked through page after page of Rachel's happy images. She used to be my closest friend, and yet I hadn't received one message from her. Knowing how close I was to my mum, it broke my heart that Rachel hadn't thought to drop me a text or email. Or even a sad emoji on social media. Did she even know Mum had died?

A fierce tightness gripped my gut, forcing all the air from my lungs. The tears flowed now, and I gripped my pillow and cried – deep, racking sobs.

"You okay, Mags?" Kenny asked from behind the door.

I sat up and wiped my tears away with my hands, gulping for breath.

The handle turned down and rattled a couple of times. But I'd pulled the new bolt in place.

"Maggie? Are you all right?"

I rolled over on the bed and placed my feet on the floor, wiping my wet hands on the satin pyjama bottoms.

"Mags. Open the door. I'm worried about you. Come on. Open the door or else I'll kick it in."

"I… I'm okay. I'm just sad, that's all."

"I know how that feels. You shouldn't be on your own right now. Neither of us should."

"Please, Kenny. Just leave me alone."

A loud thud and crack of wood splintering had me on my feet, my hands clasped to my mouth stifling a silent scream.

CHAPTER 2

Kenny burst into my room. "I don't know how many times I've told you, I won't allow locked doors under my roof. You hear me?"

I nodded. My body trembled.

He reached for my hands. "There, there, little one. It's okay, I promise you."

Silent tears spilled down my cheeks and I shuddered as he wiped a thumb across my jaw.

"Come on, Mags. We don't need to creep about anymore. We're free to do what the hell we like now."

I stumbled back, trying to get away. "No! Please, I just want to be alone. Can't you leave me to grieve for my mother in peace?"

"I can help you." He nodded and gripped my arm, yanking me forwards. "We can be a great comfort to each other."

"No. This is wrong. Please, Kenny. Please, not tonight."

"I'm lonely, Mags. I just don't want to feel lonely anymore." He dragged me from my room.

I fought like a wildcat. But with his six-four frame, and muscles, well-toned at the gym, he easily managed to drag me across the landing and into his room, scraping my bare heels along the carpet.

"Please. Not in here. Think about Mum."

"It's because of her we're in this situation, Mags. She abandoned us. She abandoned you and she abandoned me. You and I are all we have left, my love. She would want us to comfort each other."

"Not like this, she wouldn't," I spat.

He seized me by the shoulders and shoved me onto his bed. "I wonder how she'd have felt if she'd known all the nights you came on to me while she lay dying in the room below."

"I didn't... It wasn't me. I would never..."

"Oh, I suppose you're going to blame me. I'm a red-blooded male and there you are, soaping yourself down seductively in the shower. Teasing me. Taunting me. What did you expect me to do?"

"I didn't even know you were there. You took the lock off the bathroom door and came in without me knowing."

"Ah. So that's how you justify your behaviour, is it?"

I shook my head, feeling my chest tighten. "I didn't. You know it wasn't like that."

He began to unbuckle his belt. "All those nights you begged me for more, couldn't get enough of it, could you, you little slut."

I knew there was no point arguing. Nobody would believe me over him, he was such a good liar. He even had *me* thinking it may have been my fault.

He approached the bed, unfastening his trousers. "That's a good girl. You know it's much better not to fight me, don't you?"

I whimpered. My heart thundered.

He reached towards me and, hooking his fingers in my waistband, he slid my pyjama bottoms down and off.

He groaned. "You're so fucking beautiful, Mags. I can't be held responsible for what I do to you. It's human nature." He pushed his trousers down and kicked his feet out of them, then did the same with his underpants. He gripped his fist around his huge cock and rubbed it roughly. "Look at the effect you have on me. If it got any bigger it'd split the skin."

I stared at him.

At it.

Every other time had been in total darkness, so I'd never actually seen it before. I could tell you how it felt, even the taste, but not what it looked like and I almost puked. No wonder it hurt so much. "Please, Kenny. I'm begging you, don't do this."

"You need to take care of me now. You told your mum you would, didn't you?"

"Yes, but…" I whimpered again edging away from him.

"Are you trying to say this isn't what she meant?"

I nodded. "She meant cook and clean for you. Not… *this!*"

He barked out a laugh. "Of course she meant this. Your mother knew. She's always known." He tore at my top and the buttons flew off in all directions.

"Don't say that. Don't you *ever* say that again!" I screamed.

"But it's true, Mags. She turned a blind eye while I fucked and sucked her daughter because she knew I would turn to her if not."

"No!" I cried. "I don't believe you." But a tiny voice niggled at me, telling me he was maybe telling the truth.

I thought back to the earlier years. How I would hear Mum crying and begging him to stop, followed by the beatings she'd endured. The cuts and bruises she tried to hide from me, or how she made up lies to explain away the injuries she couldn't hide. But now, thinking about it, I realised those attacks on her stopped when he turned his attention to me.

He used his knees to part my legs, then he climbed on top of me and grinned. "Because she'd given birth to you, she was loose and struggled to excite me. Unlike you. Just the thought of you could have me jizzing in my pants."

His bumbling fingers went to work fiddling and poking at my privates.

My mother had explained to me about the *birds and the bees,* as she put it. She'd said men had needs and desires that were a woman's duty to satisfy, but the way she'd described it had been something beautiful. Not this.

A few months earlier, when this first began, I'd fought him. He didn't force me back then. He just fastened up his trousers and left the room. Then I would hear him beating up my mother. So, in the end, I allowed him to do his worst if it meant he'd leave Mum alone. But he couldn't hurt her anymore. So what if he threw me out onto the streets, I was old enough to leave home now. I refused to be his sex slave any longer.

I struggled against him, but I was no match physically, and he knew it. He pinned me back onto the bed and thrust himself roughly inside me.

The more I struggled, the harder he thrusted, and the deeper his fingers dug into the flesh on my arms. It seemed my discomfort excited him. Then his fingers closed about my throat and pressed down on my windpipe.

Already short of breath, my head suddenly filled with a blinding whiteness and I tried to scream at the thought that he intended to kill me. My body sagged – unable to fight him anymore. I zoned out, although still aware his fingers were prodding and groping at me and his teeth nipping at my lips and neck. It just no longer hurt.

Then, after a series of grunts, he rolled off me.

I lay still, terrified that if I moved too soon, he'd become aroused again. I didn't think I could survive another assault.

After a few minutes, his breathing changed. He was asleep.

Holding my breath, I moved barely an inch at a time, petrified of waking him. Just as I got to the edge of the bed, his heavy arm plonked on top of me and dragged me back towards him.

"Where you going?" he growled. "I haven't finished with you yet."

"I need a wee, Kenny. That's all."

"Be quick. Hurry up."

I shot from the bed as fast as my brutalized body would allow and headed to the bathroom. I lifted the toilet lid and tried to be sick but I just coughed. I'd had no appetite for any of the food in the buffet earlier.

What the hell was I going to do? He didn't intend to let me back into my own room. He hadn't finished with me yet, he'd said. I couldn't allow him to touch me again. No fucking way.

I glanced around for something to use to defend myself with, but there was nothing sharper than an eyeliner pencil in the bathroom cabinet.

"Maggie!" Kenny yelled.

I pressed my fingers to my forehead. "Coming," I replied, trying to keep my voice calm. But I knew if I went back in there without a weapon, I would have to go through the same again, and probably much worse.

I needed to put an end to this tonight, or he wouldn't allow me a minute of peace, I was sure. But first, I would have to get downstairs.

"Maggie? What the fuck?"

I appeared at his side and smiled. "I'm a little hungry, Kenny. Do you fancy a chicken sandwich?"

He rolled onto one elbow and sneered. "It's almost midnight. Eating at this hour will make you fat."

"I haven't eaten a thing all day. I feel weak."

"Hurry up, then. You're gonna need all your strength for what I have in mind for you." His snigger made my stomach lurch.

My legs moved so fast on the stairs I almost got friction burns on the soles of my feet. In the kitchen, I leaned against the sink, and took several deep breaths. Then, I opened the cupboard above the kettle and pulled out my spare inhaler. The last thing I needed right now was an asthma attack.

When I could breathe normally again, I took Kenny's filleting knife from the cutlery drawer.

Still naked, I hid the knife behind my back and turned to head upstairs. As I opened the kitchen door, I screamed and staggered backwards.

Kenny was standing in the doorway stroking his disgusting, angry looking penis. "Look what I've got waiting for you. I hope you didn't eat too much. I don't want you to gag when this is tickling your tonsils."

"Kenny. This can't happen. Mum's gone. Why don't you find yourself a new girlfriend? One of the women from today maybe? Nobody will mind."

His eyes flashed angrily and his lip curled in another sneer. "Because I don't want one of those trollops. I want you. Now come here and put a smile on your daddy's face."

"You're not my father," I spat out.

Kenny lunged at me, snatching hold of my hair and dragging me towards him, his face inches from mine. "No. Your fucking deadbeat father did a runner the first chance he got. Who's been there for you all these years? Who provided for you? Seems you have a short memory, Mags. *Who?*" Kenny yelled the last word and made me jump.

"You have. But a father wouldn't do these things. This is wrong."

"I'm fucking disappointed in you, Maggie. I thought we were finished with all this shit."

For every step away from him I took, he matched it, the sneer back on his face. I banged into the table, and terror struck me, there was no escape.

Kenny shoved me further backwards onto the table and I knew he planned to rape me again.

I lashed out, bringing the knife up as hard as I could. I roared as the blade came into contact with his bare stomach. I rammed the knife forwards with all my might. It wasn't as easy as I'd expected, all that hard muscle was tough to cut through, but I couldn't wimp out now – I knew it was him or me.

His expression went from anger to confusion as he staggered backwards. He glanced down at his stomach and then back at me, wobbled and crashed backwards to the tiles.

I'd stopped breathing.

Was he dead?

I looked down at my bloody fingers. I was still gripping the long, thin, incredibly sharp knife.

"Mags…"

The sound of his hoarse whisper made my knees almost buckle. The bastard wasn't dead.

He wasn't dead.

He wasn't dead!

I couldn't allow him to live. He'd never stop. I refused to spend the rest of my life being molested and assaulted by him.

With a strangled cry, I launched myself at him, flailing blindly with the knife until I was certain there was no chance of him surviving.

Exhausted, I dropped the knife and scrambled away on all fours. Then I sat on my bum, my arms wrapped tightly around my knees.

I don't know how long I sat there for, rocking until I heard a sound from outside. I felt revolted by the metallic tang that now filled the room.

I didn't look at him. I could just see the bluey-white skin of his legs and a large red mess from the corner of my eye. I numbly walked into the hall, picked up the phone and dialled 999.

"Police, please," I said, calmly. "My stepfather's dead. I killed him."

I gave the woman the address before ending the call. Then I padded upstairs to my room.

I heard the sirens a minute or two before they pulled up on the street outside.

I peered from the window. Two police cars and an ambulance. I wasn't sure why they'd sent the ambulance – Kenny was dead.

CHAPTER 3

I wrapped myself in a sheet and made my way down the stairs as though in a dream. Without saying a word, I led the officers through to the kitchen.

"Shit!" the first officer said, dropping to one knee beside Kenny's body.

I left them to it and staggered back upstairs where I curled up on my bed. I could hear people coming and going on the wooden stairs and a lot of chatter, but none of the words were clear.

After a while, Detective Jake Stuart knocked on the door and entered my bedroom. I'd known him for years; he and his wife were good friends of Kenny and my mother.

"Maggie? Are you all right, love?"

I didn't reply. Surely it wasn't okay for *him* to investigate. He wouldn't have a bad word to say against Kenny. Good old Kenny wouldn't harm a fly.

He crouched down beside the bed. "What did you do to him?"

I turned away and focused on my bloodstained hands.

"Come on, get dressed. You'll need to come with us."

Jake got to his feet and turned his back on me, but I could see he was ogling me in the reflection of the dressing table mirror.

"Is this what you want to see?" I screamed, dropping the sheet and flying to my feet. "Go on. Have a good look." I squeezed my boobs together and then shoved my balled fists at his back. "Get out! Get out, get out, get out!"

Jake rushed through the door.

"She's fucking lost the plot," I heard him say.

"Do you think he was fiddling with her?" another male voice said.

"No way. Not Kenny. He wasn't like that," Jake said.

"They are both naked. And a torn pyjama top is in his bedroom as well as the bottoms. I know how it looks to me."

"Lucky it's not down to you, is it, Bobby?" Jake hissed. "Now get on with your job and keep your fucking mouth buttoned – got it?"

"Yes, Sarge."

Listening to the exchange, I knew it was pointless. The whole village would believe Kenny over me. But at least I'd made the bastard pay. No matter what they did to me after this, at least *he* wasn't walking away from it.

Detective Inspector Donna Sullivan was asleep when she got the call about a homicide. It appeared the victim's daughter was responsible and they wanted a female detective to take over.

Twenty minutes later, she walked into the three-bedroomed, terraced house in the lovely village of Harley. DS Jake Stuart gave her a quick debrief.

"Maggie, his daughter, did it. She confessed when she called it in."

"Why? Do you know?"

Jake shrugged. "She's lost her marbles. She even accused me of trying to have a look at her body. She tore off the sheet she was wearing in front of me and almost shoved her tits in my face."

"Any drugs involved?"

He shook his head. "Don't think so."

Donna entered the kitchen. It seemed the daughter had done a fine number on her father. He'd been stabbed multiple times. Then, on her way up to see the suspect, Donna stepped into the master bedroom. A quick examination of the bed showed blood mixed with semen on the mattress. It was pretty obvious to her what had gone on.

She knocked and entered the girl's room, noticing the broken lock.

"Hi, Maggie. My name's DI Sullivan, but you can call me Donna."

The girl was slumped in the far corner of the room. Her dark auburn curls wild and frizzy. She didn't acknowledge Donna at all.

Donna crouched down beside her. "I'm sorry, Maggie. I know the last thing you'd want to do is answer a load of questions, but I'm going to have to take you down to the station. Will you get dressed for me, sweetheart?"

The girl looked at her with large, sad, indigo-coloured eyes and Donna's heart broke.

"Come on. It's okay. I promise." She held her hand out and Maggie allowed herself to be helped to her feet.

Maggie pulled out a pair of jeans and a T-shirt from the top drawer. She dropped the sheet and hurriedly dressed.

"You ready?" Donna asked.

Maggie nodded.

Out in the hall, Maggie flinched when she saw the number of police and SOCO that were falling over themselves in the small house.

Donna led the traumatised girl downstairs and out onto the street.

"Maggie! Maggie, what's happened, love?" An older woman, with two rollers pinned to the front of her head, tried to push her way through the police cordon but she was gruffly shoved back by a uniformed officer.

Maggie hung her head and whimpered, covering her face with her hands.

Donna put a protective arm around the girl's shoulders and guided her to the navy-blue Volvo.

They drove to the police station in silence.

"Can I get you a hot drink?" Donna asked when they were inside the interview room. "Tea? Hot chocolate?"

Maggie shook her head and continued staring at her hands, seemingly mesmerized by the blood still coating them.

"I'm just waiting for a colleague of mine to join us, and then I'll need to ask you a few questions, Maggie. Is that all right?"

A thumping on the door drowned out anything the girl may have said.

Donna saw Jake Stuart through the small square window in the door. She jumped to her feet as he walked in.

"Don't tell me – she's giving you some sob story that Kenny abused her?" he barked.

Maggie shuddered and hid her face.

"Excuse me a moment," Donna said to Maggie. She turned to shove Jake back out the door.

"What the hell's wrong with you?" she hissed when the door had closed behind them. "Don't you come in there all guns blazing, mate. I won't stand for it. Did you see the way she looked at you?"

"I don't bloody care, Ma'am. She just gutted one of my best mates with a filleting knife."

"And you're not in the least bit interested why, Detective?"

"What possible motive is there? He'd just buried his wife, for fuck's sake."

"Jake. I suggest you take a step back from this. You're a personal friend of the victim's, which is good enough reason in itself, but I will not have you intimidating the suspect. Do you hear me?"

"But…"

"I said – do you hear me, Detective?"

He lowered his head and walked away.

"Arsehole," she muttered, before heading back in the room.

"Maggie. I want to apologise for Detective Stuart. He had no right to say those things. If you'd just bear with me a second, I'll organise a cup of tea for us both and then I'll be right back. Okay?"

The girl seemed relieved Jake hadn't come back in, and with a shaky smile, she nodded.

Donna left and returned a few minutes later with another female detective and two disposable cups filled with milky tea.

"Here you go. I didn't know how you take it, but I figured hot and sweet in the circumstances."

Maggie nodded and snaked her fingers around the cup.

"This is Detective Yvette Dawson. We call her Evie."

"Hi, Maggie," Evie said, pulling a chair up to the table and making herself comfortable.

"We need to ask you a few questions, but for the record, can you confirm your name for me, please," Donna said.

Maggie nodded and cleared her throat. "Margaret Jane Simms."

Donna smiled and patted the girl's arm. "Good girl. Now, you know why we're here. You made an emergency call early this morning stating you'd killed your father."

"He's not my father," Maggie snarled.

"I see. " Donna took a deep breath. Now she had the girl

talking she didn't want to mess it up. "My mistake, sorry. Could you tell me who he was to you?"

"My mum's husband." Maggie's voice cracked at the mention of her mother.

"And, correct me if I'm mistaken, but it was your mum's funeral yesterday?"

Maggie nodded.

"Is that a *yes*?"

"Yes."

"Thank you. Now, I know it will be difficult, but can you tell me what happened last night?"

Maggie pressed her lips firmly together.

"Maybe we can talk about your mum for a while. What did she die of?"

"Cancer. Breast cancer."

"I see. And was she sick for a long time?"

Maggie's eyes filled and she shook her head.

Donna knew she should stay impartial, but she was beginning to feel an immense sadness for the girl. She got to her feet and took a box of tissues from the windowsill, placing it on the table.

Maggie pulled a couple of tissues from the box and poked at the corners of her eyes. "Just a few months. She found a lump. But when she got it checked out, it was too late."

Donna winced. "That's terrible. It must have hit you hard."

Suddenly Maggie sobbed, squeezing her eyes shut.

Feeling wretched, Donna raised her eyebrows at Evie. She waited until Maggie calmed a little before continuing. "Can you tell me about your stepfather?"

Maggie blew her nose and shrugged. "What do you want to know? He's an accountant."

"Tell me about your relationship with him."

Maggie scratched her neck, her eyebrows furrowed. "He was a bully. An ignorant pig who used to torment and beat my mother."

"Did he bully you?"

"Sometimes."

"Did he beat you?"

She shook her head. "No."

"Did he force himself on you?"

Maggie looked back down at her hands.

"Maggie, I'll tell you what I noticed as a seasoned detective, shall I?"

The girl lifted her eyes to Donna's.

"The first thing that struck me was you were both naked. Yeah, some people sleep naked, but I noticed your pyjamas were on your father's bedroom floor. I also noticed the top had been ripped off, the buttons were scattered over the floor too."

Maggie glanced at Evie then back at her hands.

"Upon examination of the bed, I saw a pool of semen mixed with blood. Your blood, I'm betting. And your bedroom door had been forced open."

Maggie wrung her hands together.

"Then, I find you, covered in blood and bruises, cowering in your bedroom. I know what's happened, Maggie. And I'm pretty certain Evie knows as well, but we will need you to tell us, love."

She shook her head. "I c-can't."

"Let me be honest with you, Maggie," Evie said. "If you don't tell us what happened, you will be charged with murder. Do you understand?"

Maggie nodded.

"That means you could get twenty-five years in prison. Is that what you want?"

Still nothing.

Evie stretched out on her chair, sighing deeply, and shaking her head in sheer frustration.

Maggie bristled at Evie's obvious displeasure.

"Maggie. What are you frightened of?" Donna asked. "Make a statement then we'll need to get you checked over by a doctor which I'm positive will corroborate what I think has happened. But, if we're to help you, you have to tell us, love."

"I can't." Tears continued to stream down her face. "Nobody will believe me. Just like Jake."

"Screw Jake," Donna said. "He's a friend of your stepfather's. His opinion doesn't count."

"Promise?"

"I promise you, Maggie. I will look after you. Jake Stuart will not be allowed to work on this case."

"Okay. I'll tell you."

***

I hadn't told them everything. Donna had been so kind but I just couldn't. What I was telling them wasn't anything they didn't already know.

I then had to have a physical examination. The grey-haired lady doctor took swabs of my privates as well as scrapings from underneath my fingernails. She also photographed all my bruises. I was terrified, but knew there was no way to avoid it. I closed my eyes and tried to block out what she was doing to me.

Then I stood under a hot shower and allowed the water to wash away Kenny's stench from my body.

***

Back in the interview room, Donna sat me down again.

"Now, don't be alarmed, Maggie, but I'm going to have to charge you with manslaughter. However, considering the evidence we have, I'm certain the charges will be dropped. Do you understand?"

I nodded. "Will I go to prison?"

"I'll call the duty solicitor shortly. Hopefully you should be released on bail later on today."

"But where will I go?"

"You don't have any other family?"

I shook my head. "No, none."

"Who's the woman who called over to you when we left the house?"

"Claudia Green. Our next-door neighbour. She's lovely."

"She's been in reception since you arrived. She clearly cares about you. Do you think you could go back with her?"

I nodded. "Possibly."

"Okay, let's get the technicalities over with, and then I'll go and have a chat with her for you, all right?"

I nodded. I was so tired, I hadn't slept since the day before Mum's funeral and then only briefly.

When I'd been formally charged, my fingerprints were taken and then Donna apologised as she put me in a cell.

I was so relieved I didn't have to share it with anybody else. It was just a bare room with a bare mattress and a stainless steel sink and toilet.

Donna handed me a blanket. "Try to get a little sleep. I'll come back with an update soon."

CHAPTER 4

There was no chance of getting any sleep, my brain was on fire. I kept going over and over things in my mind. Kenny had blamed me – said I was a tease. Had I been? If I had, I didn't mean to be. He'd been all I had left. Now I had nobody. Not a soul. And I had no means to support myself. But that was the least of my worries, really. After what Jake said earlier, I could see I would have a fight on my hands. Kenny was popular. A man's man. A ladies man too, apparently.

What if they found me guilty? I could end up in jail for years.

The only positive thing to come out of it was putting an end to Kenny's abuse. I hadn't told the detectives everything. As far as they knew, last night had been the first time Kenny had touched me. At least then nobody could blame my dear mother. I didn't give a shit what Kenny had said, there was no way she would have allowed him to lay one finger on me. I was certain of that. If it meant his lies had died with him, I was glad I'd shut him up. I'd do it all over again in a heartbeat.

Donna completed her paperwork and then called to arrange a duty solicitor. She was relieved when the operator put her through to Matt Pierson, a relatively new and passionate solicitor. She knew that, unlike his colleagues, Matt preferred pro-bono cases. He'd worked his arse off to get where he was. Born on the Ordsall estate in Salford, he knew how it felt to go without. And instead of making him greedy, now he could afford a few luxuries in life, he preferred to help less fortunate people instead.

"Oh, Matt. I was hoping it would be you."

"Hi Donna. Why, what have you got for me?"

"A sixteen-year-old girl, Maggie Simms. She knifed her stepfather to death last night. He'd raped her."

"Okay, I'll finish up here and be with you within the hour."

"Great. See you then."

True to his word, Matt strode into her office forty minutes later and placed his briefcase on her desk.

Donna handed him the file she'd just been working on. "Take a look at that while I fetch us a cuppa. Tea okay?"

"Perfect." He pulled up a chair and opened the folder.

When she returned with two steaming mugs, he looked up and smiled sadly. "Sometimes I despair at what human beings put each other through. Fancy just burying your mother and then having to endure such an attack from your only remaining family member." He ran a hand through his gingery-blond hair.

"I know. Only, between you and me, I have a feeling last night wasn't the first time."

"Did she say that?"

Donna shook her head, her mouth turned down at the corners. "No. But you don't work for years in a job like this without developing a sixth sense."

"I guess not. But, looking at this evidence, we shouldn't need to humiliate the poor girl any more than necessary."

"That's what I figured. Are you ready to meet her?"

"Whenever you are."

They finished their drinks and Donna led him to the interview room before going to fetch Maggie from the cell.

Donna found the girl sitting on the edge of the bed as though she hadn't moved in hours.

"The duty solicitor's here to see you, Maggie. Hopefully, when he's done his bit, you'll be able to go home."

"Home?"

Donna could have bitten her tongue off. "Sorry, love. I meant you can leave this place. I spoke to Claudia Green a while ago and she's more than happy for you to go home with her. She's gone off to prepare your room."

Maggie nodded. "Okay, thanks. Will I be allowed in my house? I'll need my things."

"It's still a crime scene I'm afraid, but we should be able to get some of your belongings for now. Enough to tide you over at least."

They headed to the interview room where Donna introduced Maggie and Matt. She left, to give them some privacy.

After the initial formalities, the solicitor took a seat opposite me and clicked open his brown leather briefcase.

"Firstly, I'd like to offer you my condolences for the death of your mother. That's a terrible thing to have to deal with, without all this added stuff."

I swallowed down a sudden surge of bile and nodded. "Thank you."

"Now, I've read the file and as far as I'm concerned, it's a straightforward case of self-defence. The police won't contest bail. I believe Detective Sullivan has spoken to your neighbour, Mrs Claudia Green, and she's happy for you to stay with her for a while. Is that okay with you?"

"What choice do I have?"

"We could speak to Social Services and see if we can find accommodation in a crisis centre or women's refuge."

I didn't want to go into a kid's home. I'd read awful things about kid's homes. "No, it's okay. I'm happy to stay with Claudia, for now."

"The thing is, if we apply for bail, it's likely there will be conditions. A nominated address will probably be one of them. So wherever you choose to go, you will need to stay there until the court date."

I shrugged. "Okay. If that's all right with Claudia. I've nowhere else to go."

"Leave it with me, then. I'll be back as soon as I can."

He left and Donna reappeared moments later. She took me back to the cell to wait.

I hadn't slept the night before. I was beginning to feel dizzy and my eyes stung. I pulled out the blanket Donna had given me and snuggled down on the hard vinyl mattress.

The events of the last few days played over in my mind as I drifted off to sleep. The loss of my mum had been bad enough, but to have to deal with everything else without her telling me I was going to be all right, made me feel lost and vulnerable. I had nobody but Claudia in the whole wide world.

The sound of the door unlocking made me force my eyes open. I struggled to sit up, expecting Matt or Donna to be bearing good news. But my heart dropped to the cold concrete floor when I saw Jake.

"Nice to see you're catching up on your sleep, young lady." He sneered. "God forbid you'd feel a little guilty or anything."

My ears felt hot and a pounding began in my head. "I... I haven't slept since it happened."

"Another lie – you're becoming quite the expert. I looked through the slot before I came in. You were out for the count."

"What do you want, Jake? Where's Donna?" I meant for my voice to be strong, but it sounded the opposite.

"Donna? She's not your friend, or how do the kids say it nowadays? BFF? She's DI Sullivan to you. And I'm DS Stuart – got it?"

I gulped and nodded, suddenly aware of a warm sensation in my pants and down my legs. I was horrified as I realised I'd peed myself.

Jake jumped backwards, an amused expression on his face as he looked at the puddle surrounding me on the floor.

"You have no business being in here, Detective," Donna said, suddenly appearing in the doorway.

"I was just checking on our guest. Seeing if she needed anything, wasn't I, Mags?" He glared at me defiantly.

"Don't call me that," I snarled.

He arched one eyebrow, clearly amused. "Seems I hit a nerve. Anyway, I was a little too late, by the looks of things. Your guest has just relieved herself all over the floor."

"Leave, Detective," Donna snarled, "or I shall have no choice but to lodge a formal complaint."

Jake held his hands up and backed out of the cell. "Be seeing you – *Mags.*"

I was seething. The only person who called me Mags had been Kenny. But I was more annoyed with myself for letting Jake know it bothered me.

"Come on. Let's get you cleaned up."

The humiliation caused my cheeks to flush. "I'm sorry."

"Hey. It's fine."

She led me to the toilet and told me to get undressed, then she handed me a pair of overalls over the top of the cubicle.

"Better?" she asked as I stepped into the corridor.

"Much better. Thanks."

"Don't mention it." She stroked my arm. "I've got good news. You're free to go. Your neighbour has been informed and is on her way over to pick you up."

Tears suddenly filled my eyes and spilled over onto my cheeks.

I'd been certain she was going to come back and tell me I was going to prison instead.

Ten minutes later, I'd been read all the bail conditions by the Desk Sergeant, collected my belongings, and escorted to the main entrance. "Thanks for everything," I said to Donna. "When can I get some of my things from the house?"

"If you can make do for tonight, I'll come over first thing." She gave me a half smile and was still watching me when I looked back at her from the doorway a minute later.

CHAPTER 5

"Oh, there you are, duck. I've been beside myself," Claudia said as she hauled herself from the faded green BMW she'd owned as far back as I could remember.

I didn't talk. Seeing the sympathy in her eyes brought a rush of emotion and it settled as a huge ball in my throat.

"Come on, let's get you home. Sandy's more than a little anxious as to who we're expecting." Sandy was her scruffy but cute little dog that she treated like a human.

Maybe I'd need to get a Sandy equivalent now I had nobody else, a little dog to love me unconditionally. It was a terrifying thought for a sixteen year old to consider – to be totally alone. I was grateful for Claudia, but I knew she was helping me from a sense of decency – nothing more.

Five minutes into the twenty-minute journey, Claudia startled me from my daydream. "Steak and kidney pie for tea. Is that all right?"

I nodded and turned to stare out of the window at the huge, imposing city buildings. The thought of food made me want to hurl. I would need to enlist Sandy to help me out when Claudia wasn't watching.

When we turned onto our street, my heart almost stopped.

Blue and white police tape had been stretched across the doorway of my house in the shape of a huge X.

I started to cry as I stared at the only home I'd ever known. A tightness in my chest prevented me taking a breath and I became lightheaded.

Claudia rushed around the car and yanked my door open. "Come on, I've got you." She eased me from the car and, with a protective arm around my shoulders, led me to the house next door.

Sandy launched himself down the narrow staircase and performed a series of twirls when he saw us.

"Not now, you little show off. Go on, go and lie down."

I laughed a little through my snotty tears as the silly dog turned dejectedly and skulked up the hall and into the kitchen.

"That's better. Sandy never fails to cheer me up when I'm feeling low too." Claudia led me through to the peachy coloured lounge room and settled me down onto the sofa. "Now, put your feet up and I'll make us a nice cup of tea, and I'm sure I could rustle up a slice of Madeira cake, if you're hungry."

"Thank you," I managed as she got to the door.

Claudia wasn't as overpowering as I'd expected. She showed me to her cosy spare bedroom, which was the mirror image of my room next door, except the woodchip wallpaper had had so many coats of pink paint that it looked almost flat. She told me to make myself at home and when I hadn't appeared by dinnertime, she brought a huge portion of steak and kidney pie, mashed potatoes and broccoli up to my room.

I had no choice but to eat the food, considering Sandy was still downstairs.

At around eleven p.m., I heard Claudia climb the stairs and go into her bedroom. I sat up as the sliver of light coming under my door suddenly went out, and I reached to turn on the bedside lamp.

A feeling of emptiness washed over me, and I wasn't sure if I felt sick or hungry. I tiptoed from my bed and out onto the landing. I could hear Sandy snuffling behind Claudia's bedroom door and I hoped he wouldn't bark.

In the bathroom, I splashed my face with cold water and brushed my teeth with a spare toothbrush Claudia had left out for me. The growling in my stomach was almost painful, so I padded downstairs to the kitchen. In the fridge I found a plastic container filled with sliced ham, and before I knew it, I'd devoured the lot. I almost cried when I noticed the empty container and guiltily washed it up, hoping Claudia wouldn't notice.

I downed a glass of water, and grabbed a packet of crisps from a cupboard before scurrying back up to my bedroom. But even when I'd eaten the chips, the gnawing emptiness remained.

The single bed was the comfiest I'd ever slept in, although the bed frame clanged every time I moved. Thankfully, I managed to get a good night's sleep.

The next morning, Donna came around as promised.

"I don't think it's a good idea, Detective," Claudia said. "I'm presuming the house is still in a mess. " She raised her eyebrows, nodding at me, clearly meaning Kenny's blood.

I rolled my eyes. Claudia wasn't the most tactful of people, but her heart was in the right place.

"I promise you, I'll take her straight up the stairs into her room. We'll be back before you know it."

Claudia stomped from the room, stony faced.

"I need to have a word with you about something else," Donna said to me when we were alone.

"What about?"

"Veronica and Valerie Simms. Kenny's sisters."

"Ah." I nodded in acknowledgment. I'd heard all about them over the years, but I'd never actually met them. Kenny didn't have a lot of time for them.

"They've claimed their brother's body, but I get the impression they're only interested in how much money they'll be entitled to. Maggie, did your mum leave a will, do you know?"

I shrugged. "Doubt it. Why?"

"I'm pretty sure the law states you cannot be the beneficiary of a will of somebody you killed. Did you know that?"

I shrugged again. "I didn't, but I don't want anything of his anyway. What about my mum's stuff though? Can I have that?"

"It's not up to me, I'm afraid. You need to talk to your solicitor to see what your rights are. I just wanted to warn you they were sniffing around."

"Are they angry with me? What if they come here?"

"I didn't get that impression. Plus they don't know where you are. If they do turn up and you feel threatened, call 999. I'll tag your number as high priority." She got to her feet. "Right, are you sure you're up to this?"

I nodded, standing up.

Claudia came out of the kitchen when she saw us in the hall. "I'd rather you tell me what you want and I can go in instead."

"Thanks, Claudia. But I'll be fine."

She rubbed my arm.

"I'll be fine." I smiled. "Honestly, I'll just grab a few bits and I'll be back out."

She walked us to the front door, wringing a tea towel in her hands.

I kept a smile of bravado on my face until she was out of view, but my stomach clenched as I stepped into my childhood home.

Echoes of the past made me gasp as thousands of wonderful memories of my mother flashed through my mind, all rolled into one. There had been a lot of laughter. Even though Kenny had made her miserable towards the end, things hadn't always been that way. I turned to Donna and shook my head. "Don't know if I can do this."

Donna nodded. "Tell me what you want and I'll get them for you."

I shrugged. "I don't even know what I want. Just a few clothes."

"Okay, I'll grab what I can. Hang on there."

I backed up along the hallway and leaned against the front door. It no longer felt like home. It was cold. Like the heart of the house had died along with my mum. The gnawing emptiness in my stomach returned, and I was unsure if I wanted to eat or vomit.

"Okay, I emptied your chest of drawers into this bag I found in the wardrobe," Donna said, trudging down the stairs carrying a dark blue holdall in front of her. "Are you okay?"

I nodded. "What will happen with this place now?"

Donna's eyebrows crinkled as she looked at me with pity. "You can't benefit from his death, you *do* understand that, don't you?"

"Yeah, you told me. But what will happen to it?"

"If your stepdad made a will, his belongings will be divvied up between the benefactors, I'm guessing."

"So, not only will Kenny's nasty sisters inherit my mum's house, but they'll get all her things too?"

Donna shrugged. "It's nothing to do with me, I'm sorry. You'll need to ask Matt."

I took the holdall from her and threw the straps over my shoulder. "Thanks for this." I managed a smile.

We headed back next door.

Donna left soon after and I went up to my room to call the solicitor.

"Hi, Matt. It's Maggie Simms."

"Hello, Maggie. I was just about to call you."

"Really? What about?"

"I'll need to go through your statement and get everything clear in my mind. Do you want to come into my office or shall I meet you somewhere?"

"I'll come to you, if that's okay?"

"Perfect. Shall we make it for, say... one p.m.?"

Yes. That's fine – where are you?"

"Mercury Lane in the city. We're on the third floor of the huge green building opposite the gym."

I nodded. "Great, see you then."

Now all I needed to do was arrange to actually get there.

Claudia insisted on driving me, saying she needed to do some shopping anyway, but I knew she was pretending. I did appreciate all her help, although I was under no illusion things couldn't stay this way for long. I had no choice but to find a job – and soon.

CHAPTER 6

Claudia dropped me off at the front doors and I followed the signs for Wells and Butterworth on the third floor.

I gave my name to the receptionist and took a seat on a plush brown sofa while I waited.

Matt Pierson appeared a few minutes later and shook my hand enthusiastically before leading the way to his small, tastefully furnished office.

"Okay, Maggie. How are you feeling today?"

I nodded. "Fine, I suppose."

He folded his hands in front of him on the desk. "I guess you saw last night's *Manchester Evening News*?"

"Yeah. Claudia tried to hide it from me, but I insisted she let me read it. She treats me like a kid, but I'm nearly seventeen, you know."

"I'm sure she was just trying to protect you. So, how did it feel, reading all the things they're saying about your stepfather?"

I shrugged. "I expected it. Those people didn't know what he was really like. He had a lot of fake friends."

"Fake friends?" Matt tilted his head as though confused.

"Yeah. You know. The type who pretend to be your best mate,

but only when they want something. Kenny was an accountant and would always help these people out with their tax returns, and stuff. To them, he was a great bloke."

"I see. Chances are a lot of these so-called mates will probably speak up for him in court. And although, in my opinion, this case is cut and dried, witnesses of their calibre will have a lot of clout."

"You mean the judge will believe them?"

"There's no way of knowing. That's why we need to have all our i's dotted and t's crossed, just in case."

"I wanted to ask you something. How can I pay Claudia for having me? How am I supposed to support myself? I don't have a job. I'm still in school, officially."

"I'm sure Social Services will be in touch with Mrs Green. She'll be able to claim a benefit for having you stay with her."

"She won't want to be lumbered with me forever, though."

"Did she say that?"

"No. But it's obvious, isn't it? You wouldn't want a sixteen-year-old rocking up to your doorstep and staying forever, would you?"

"Depends on who it was. Mrs Green was close to your mother, by all accounts."

"That doesn't mean she wants to be responsible for me."

"No, I know that, but I think you need to give her the chance to make up her own mind."

"The detective told me I wasn't able to claim any of my mother's things because I killed Kenny."

"Yes. The law is in place to stop people getting tired of waiting for their inheritance and bumping off their benefactors. But, it's not very helpful in a case like this, I'm afraid. Who's your parents' solicitor? Do you know?"

I shook my head. "All I want are a few of my mum's things – they'll mean nothing to anybody else."

"I'll make a few calls – find out some more details. But I think you need to prepare yourself for bad news, I'm afraid."

I nodded and looked down at my hands, a twisted mass of fingers, on my lap.

Matt opened up a file on his desk and asked me things about my family. I told him all I'd told Donna, in detail, and he wrote it all down.

"Was your mum aware of what he was doing to you, Maggie?"

I gasped and whipped my head up to stare at him, trying to steady my raging heartbeat. "No. Why would she? She was dead."

Matt lifted his eyes to mine, and placed his pen on top of the file. "Maggie. I need you to trust me. Do you think you can do that?"

I gulped, and tears pricked at my eyes. I couldn't bear the thought of the world finding out my dear mother knew what the rotten bastard had been doing to me. I'd take that part to the grave. And besides, I only had Kenny's nasty insinuations to go on. They were probably lies. But I needed to tell Matt something. He knew I was keeping something from him, and would just continue to hound me if I didn't tell him more.

I shook my head, poking my fingers at the corners of my eyes. "She didn't know anything. I kept it from her."

"But it *had* happened before?"

I nodded.

"When did it begin?"

I opened my mouth to speak, but instead deep sobs escaped me and I doubled over and allowed myself to cry. I was just sixteen, my mum had died and I'd been charged with killing my stepfather. I had no money and no family and no prospects, so the tears didn't need much coaxing.

After a few minutes, I fought to get myself under control. I wiped my eyes and my nose on the sleeve of my jacket and nodded. "It started around four months ago, after Mum became sick."

Matt got to his feet and came to my side, handing me a wad of tissues. "It's okay, Maggie. It's okay." He rubbed my shoulder gently. "Kenny was a despicable human being for preying on an innocent child."

"But I'm not a child. Not according to the law. I'm sixteen and therefore legally allowed to have sex."

"But you didn't have sex, did you? He raped you. That's illegal no matter what your age."

"He said I egged him on. That it was all my fault."

"Listen, Maggie. That's what all rapists tell their victims. They try to justify their actions, minimise the severity of the attacks. They'll try to make you believe the way the victim may have dressed or behaved was to blame."

"That's what he said to me. I knew everyone would believe him – he *was* good old Kenny, after all."

"So, what made you…?"

"What made me kill him?" I sobbed. "Because it was never gonna end. I let him use me when Mum was alive to stop him from hurting her. But when she was gone, I didn't have to do it anymore. But instead of him finding himself a new wife or girl-friend, he said we could be together properly. He even wanted me to do it in her bed. And he was rough, too. Really rough."

"It was clear he raped you in your bedroom, but how did you end up in the kitchen?"

"I managed to get out of bed when he fell asleep. I needed my inhaler. I'm asthmatic, you see. The next thing I knew he was behind me, in the kitchen. Ready for round two. I was terrified. I opened the drawer and grabbed the first knife I could find."

Matt noisily sucked in air over his teeth. "So you could see no way out?"

"No. None." I retrieved my inhaler from my pocket and took two deep pulls on it.

"Is that better?"

I nodded. "For now."

Matt was seething as he listened to Maggie's heart-wrenching confession. But he wasn't surprised. This kind of thing was becoming more common nowadays. He'd done some research into Kenneth Simms, and he was, by all accounts, a stand up, likeable guy. The write-up in the paper had several prominent businessmen singing his praises, and condemning Maggie for what she'd done. But the bastard deserved everything he got, in Matt's opinion.

"I think you're extremely brave, you know? And I promise to do all I can for you."

"But I can't pay you. I've got nothing."

"Don't worry about that for now. I'll do all I can on legal aid and if it won't cover it, I'll speak to my bosses. We do several pro-bono cases a year."

"I don't know what that means?"

"It means non-profit. I would represent you for free."

When Maggie had left, Matt made a list of people to visit. The closest person to the family as far as he could tell was Mrs Green. Then there were Maggie's schoolteachers. He wanted to see if they could shed any light or if they'd suspected anything was going on. He knew they needed to balance the scales – several well thought of teachers standing up for Maggie wouldn't hurt her case.

CHAPTER 7

A few days later, I was surprised to receive a call from Matt.

"Hi, Maggie. Are you home?" He sounded really happy.

I looked up at Claudia, who was sitting across from me, sewing, and I nodded. I still couldn't get used to calling the house next door to mine 'home'. "Yes. Why?"

"I can't tell you over the phone. I'll be there in twenty minutes."

"That's odd," I said, placing the phone on the coffee table between us.

"What is?"

"Matt, my solicitor, is on his way over. He sounded like he was going to burst with excitement."

"Let's hope the charges against you have been dropped. It's a bloody outrage."

Claudia had been fuming since I told her everything, on the way home a few days earlier. I figured it would all be out in the open soon enough anyway and needed to give her the option to ask me to leave beforehand. I needn't have worried. In fact, she'd been more supportive than I'd expected and was livid Kenny had got away with everything for so long.

We heard a car pull up in the street. A familiar tightness took over my chest. I reached in my pocket for my inhaler and sucked on it.

"It'll be all right, duck. Don't get yourself all wound up." Claudia folded the tablecloth she was embroidering, and got to her feet. She straightened her pale blue dress and headed to the front door.

Matt was alone and he still had the air of someone who might burst a blood vessel if he didn't blurt out what he had to say. He sat beside me on the sofa.

"Do you want me to…?" Claudia pointed at the kitchen.

"It's up to Maggie."

They both looked at me. "No, don't be silly. I've got nothing to hide."

Claudia smiled and returned to her seat.

"I've got some fantastic news, Maggie."

"Okay." I was feeling light headed, and held onto the seat cushion to steady myself.

"I checked into your stepfather's estate and it seems all his belongings will go to his sisters."

"Yes. I guessed that."

"So I checked into your mother's will, hoping she would have left you something specific."

Bubbles of excitement began in the pit of my stomach, and I shuffled in my seat, hardly able to contain myself.

"I discovered that you were left all her personal belongings to do with as you wish."

My heartbeat thudded. "Really?"

He nodded. His eyes sparkling.

"So the law won't prevent me from inheriting off her?"

"No. Your mother had already passed and she'd made this will years ago."

"I never thought she'd have done a will."

"But, there's more." He grinned.

"Really?" I shook my head, hardly able to take it all in.

"It seems, your grandparents left the house and twenty thousand pounds in your name when they died fifteen years ago."

"I... I don't understand." I looked at Claudia, who was staring at us both, her mouth open.

"The house never belonged to your stepfather. It never even belonged to your mum."

I couldn't believe it. "Why didn't she tell me?"

"Who knows? Maybe she was waiting until you came of age."

"And I have some money too?"

"Yes. But it's in a trust until you reach your twentieth birthday, although, if you needed to, you could ask the trustees to release some of the funds for certain items in the meantime."

"I can't believe it." I shook my head.

"I think it's a marvellous result," Claudia said. "We just need you to play a blinder and get these charges dropped now, young man."

"Believe me, Mrs Green. I'm doing all I can. But in the meantime, I could murder a cup of tea."

Claudia chuckled and got to her feet. "Your wish is my command."

I was still in shock. So I wasn't homeless or penniless after all. Had Mum even told Kenny he wouldn't inherit everything? I doubted it as he'd definitely have had something to say. Maybe I could continue my education after all. Claudia had already made an appointment with somebody to apply for some money. She said she didn't mind me staying as long as I wanted, but maybe that would all change now she knew I wasn't as badly off as we'd all thought.

The next day, while helping Claudia transfer groceries from the car, a blue four by four pulled up.

I ignored it, grabbed several bags, and followed Claudia inside.

It was when Claudia went back out for the last of the bags that I heard raised voices.

Unable to face what was going on outside, I rushed upstairs to peer from my bedroom window. My pulse hammered at the sides of my head as I pulled the curtain back. My nerves had been so tightly wound recently; I knew it wouldn't take much for me to have a meltdown.

Two large, moon-faced women were standing in front of Claudia, their hands on their hips. I realised they were Kenny's sisters.

"First she murders our baby brother in cold blood, and then she steals his property," the larger woman, with wavy brown hair, said.

"I think you need to get back in your fancy car, and piss off!" Claudia said. "I was a good friend of Emily's and she told me all about you two."

"That trollop didn't even know us. What did she say?"

I grabbed my phone. If they didn't leave soon, I would call the police.

"She didn't need to know you. Why would she want to when your own brother couldn't stand the sight of you?"

The other woman, who'd been standing quietly, stepped forward and grabbed at her sister's arm. "Leave it, Vee. It's not worth getting into a slanging match over."

"Listen to your sister and go! You're not welcome round here." Claudia was just out of view, but I saw her hand rise up and point up the street. For such a gentle and caring woman, she certainly could turn on the terror when she wanted to.

The women made their way to the car, both scowling. They clambered their oversized backsides inside and sped off.

I slumped down on my bed and began breathing again.

"All clear, duck!" Claudia called up the stairs.

I forced myself upright on shaky legs and trudged down to meet her.

"Cheeky bloody bitches," she ranted as I entered the kitchen.

"You were fantastic. Remind me not to get on the wrong side of you!" I grinned, my whole body trembling.

"I don't make a habit of behaving like a fishwife, but they asked for it."

"I'm glad Mum had told you all about them. Nasty bitches."

Claudia shook her head. "Ah, but she didn't. I wouldn't have wasted my time talking about the likes of them."

"Then how...?" I cocked a thumb towards the street.

"I guessed. Let's face it. I've lived next door to the man for the past eight years and never heard him mention any sisters. You don't need to be a mind reader to know they didn't get on."

Laughter grumbled in my stomach and ruptured into a full-on belly laugh. It felt good to laugh, it had been too long. I couldn't even remember the last time.

Claudia laughed so hard she had to stop putting away the groceries to press a hand to the side of her stomach as though she had a stitch.

"You really saw them off!" I said. "Their faces, when they got back in the car, were a picture."

"Let's hope they think twice before they come back around here laying down the law."

"Something tells me they won't be back."

A few days later, I agreed to walk to the corner shop. Claudia had been urging me to get out of the house and go into the village for days. She made out the world might end as she'd run out of her favourite surface cleaner. I wasn't stupid, but I figured she was right – I couldn't stay indoors for the whole of the holidays.

I passed a few neighbours, who either smiled and waved, or hurriedly turned and entered their houses, but I could cope with that. I was just relieved they didn't fire insults or accusations at me.

Yazz, the beautiful Indian shopkeeper, smiled as I entered the shop.

"Hello, my dear. How are you today?"

I nodded. "I'm fine, thanks." I glanced about, spotting three other people in the shop. My heart stopped as I realised one of them was Rachel, my ex-best friend.

"Hi," Rachel said as I approached, a small smile lifting the corners of her mouth.

"Hi, Rach. Nice tan. How's things? I saw your lovely holiday photos on Facebook."

Her cheeks flushed. "Oh, did you? I'm sorry about the timing. With us being away, I hadn't realised the date."

It saddened me the way she seemed to bristle slightly. She was clearly uncomfortable she'd bumped into me. I shook my head, dismissing the fact that her actions had hurt me deeply. "That's okay. Life goes on, or so I'm told." I tried to smile, but I could tell by her expression I hadn't quite managed it.

"I heard about Kenny. I was shocked. Are you okay?"

"I will be." I nodded, biting my lower lip.

"Talk on the street was you were going to be banged up for years. I'm glad they were wrong."

I shrugged again. "If it hadn't been for the detective and my solicitor, I probably would have been. And, in any case, they could still be right. I need to convince the court now."

Rachel's phone rang and, startled, she looked at the screen. "We'll have to catch up properly soon. I must get off. Mum's waiting for some milk. She's dying for a proper cup of English tea." Rachel's hand flew to her mouth as she realised what she'd said. "Oh, I'm sorry, Maggie. I didn't mean…"

"Don't worry about it. I knew what you meant."

She lifted up the milk and shrugged. "Better go."

Immense sadness descended on me as I watched her walk to

the counter and then scoot out the door – clearly relieved to get away from me. We'd been so close just a few months earlier.

I picked up the cleaner Claudia wanted and also headed to the counter.

"So sorry to hear of your troubles, Maggie," Yazz said with a sad smile. "If ever you need a friend, remember I'm here. I used to have some real heart to hearts with your mum, you know."

That surprised me. I knew my mum was popular, but I hadn't realised she had any *close* friends other than Claudia. "Really?"

"Yes. And don't worry – I know what that horrible man was really like."

I gasped, tears pricking my eyes.

Shuffling of feet and a cough behind me made me jump. I placed the money on the counter. "Just this, please." Then I rushed for the door.

So Mum had confided in Yazz. How strange. Mum had been such a private person, always smiling on the outside. But she'd clearly found an ally in the soft-spoken woman.

I needed to tell Matt. Maybe he would be able to convince her to speak up for me in court.

I turned onto our street and was surprised when a silver car slowed and stopped beside me. My heart missed a beat as I watched the window wind down.

"What do we have here then?" Jake Stuart said.

"I... I've just been to the shop, Detective."

He pushed his sunglasses to the top of his head and raised one eyebrow. "Cleaner, hey?" He sneered. "Did you buy that to wash out your lying mouth by any chance?"

It took a few seconds for his words to sink in. My body began to shake uncontrollably. I shook my head and opened my mouth to speak, but nothing came out.

"You all right, Maggie?" Claudia suddenly appeared on the doorstep and I almost collapsed with relief.

Jake put his car into gear and dropped his glasses back in place before speeding off.

Tears flowed hot and fast down my cheeks.

Claudia was beside me in an instant and, placing a supportive arm around my shoulders, ushered me into the house.

She was fuming when I told her what Jake had said and she immediately grabbed her phone and began to call Donna.

"No, don't. He'll be livid if we get him in trouble. He'll get tired of picking on me eventually." I wish I could believe the words that left my mouth, they sounded believable even to my own ears.

"What made you so wise, Maggie?" Claudia said, ending the call.

I shrugged. "I'm not. But I know I can't stay around here if I want to put all this behind me."

"It's still early days. Let's see what the next few weeks bring."

———

Look at her, smiling at that old hag as though she hasn't a care in the world. Not for long. She'll pay – they'll all pay for what she's done.

CHAPTER 8

Matt contacted a few of Maggie's teachers, which had proven difficult considering it was the summer holidays.

Brenda Fellows was her form teacher and he arranged to meet her at a coffee shop in Stockport. He knew it was her as soon as she walked in. Her no-nonsense brown, knee-length skirt, cream silk blouse, and sensible shoes gave the game away. Her thick mousy-brown hair had no shape and was parted to the side and she wasn't wearing a stroke of makeup.

Matt jumped to his feet and introduced himself. "What can I get you to drink?"

"Just a black coffee, please."

He nodded. Not surprised in the least.

After ordering a coffee for her and a hot chocolate for himself, they settled across from each other.

"Now, you were asking about Maggie Simms?" Brenda said, not wasting any time on small talk.

"Yes. Yes, that's right. I just need to get an idea of what she was like before her mother was taken ill."

"Delightful. She was one of the top students in her class. I can't remember ever having a cross word with her – which is rare, I can tell you, in this day and age."

"I can imagine. Was she popular?"

Brenda looked down at her fingernails, her eyebrows tightly knitted as though deep in thought. "She wasn't unpopular – if that makes sense? But she was too considerate and gentle to be in with the most popular girls in her year."

"Did you notice a change in her behaviour at all?"

She nodded. "I did, and I feel terrible now for not digging deeper. I put it down to her mum's illness, but it's not my place to surmise anything."

"In what way did you see a change?"

"She became sullen and withdrawn. She lost weight, her uniform practically hung off her already slight frame. Classic signals that something was seriously wrong at home. She was the topic of many staffroom discussions and not one of us questioned what could be wrong. Her mum was dying, after all."

"It's not your fault, Ms Fellows. Anybody would have jumped to the same conclusion."

"I know." She nodded, sadly. "I keep telling myself the same thing, but I can't shake the feeling that I let her down."

"Would you consider being a character witness for her?"

"Of course. Although I can only state the facts. Her behaviour may well have been due to her mother's illness, when all's said and done."

"Just the truth. That's all I'm asking."

"Then yes. I will gladly be her character witness."

Afterwards, Matt met up with two more of Maggie's teachers – Charlotte Hamlett, her drama teacher, and John Taylor, her maths teacher. They said more or less the same as Ms Fellows; model student prior to her mother's diagnosis and a shadow of her former self afterwards.

Matt was well aware the prosecution would make mincemeat of their statements. Of course Maggie would appear withdrawn and sullen at school knowing what her dear mother was going through at home.

They'd also observed that, during breaks, Maggie had withdrawn herself from her usual crowd of friends, including her best friend Rachel Mendoza.

When he got back to the office, Matt called Rachel's home number. Her mother answered, almost immediately.

"Hi, Mrs Mendoza. My name is Matt Pierson. I'm Maggie Simms' solicitor."

"What are you calling here for, Mr Pierson?" she snapped.

"I was hoping to speak to your daughter, Rachel. I need some insight into how Maggie was prior to her mother's death."

"Out of the question. Rachel hadn't been friends with Maggie for weeks before her mother died."

"Can I ask you what happened? They were best friends prior to that, weren't they?"

"They just grew apart. They're kids – that's what kids do."

"Yeah, if they were ten or eleven, maybe. But not sixteen and seventeen. Most people stay in touch with their childhood friends all their lives."

"Okay. If you want to know the truth. Rachel stopped hanging around with Maggie for no other reason than she was boring."

"Boring?" Matt saw red. "Boring! I would hope if *you'd* been diagnosed with terminal cancer that your daughter wouldn't feel like *acting the goat*. That young girl has been through hell, and her supposed best friend was nowhere to be seen. What does that tell you about your precious daughter, Mrs Mendoza? Now I'm going to hang up before I say something I'll regret." He slammed the handset back on its cradle much harder than necessary, then again and again.

A few minutes later, the phone rang.

"It's Deborah Mendoza. You can call around to speak to Rachel this afternoon, on one condition. I don't want you upsetting her. Take it or leave it."

"I'll be there in a couple of hours."

At two p.m., Matt knocked on the door of a huge detached stone house. The door was opened by a glamorous woman who appeared to be in her forties.

"Ah, Mr Pierson, come on in." She led Matt through the impressive house. "Rachel's in the conservatory." Deborah threw over her shoulder as she walked. "She understands the importance of talking to you, but I'm sure you can imagine how nervous she is."

"Of course, Mrs Mendoza. I promise I won't upset her."

He followed the woman through the plush lounge and into a large rectangular conservatory.

Rachel Mendoza, an attractive young woman with shoulder-length straight brown hair, sat on a cane chair, her hands knotted in her lap.

"Hi, Rachel. Thanks for seeing me."

"Take a seat, Mr Pierson," Mrs Mendoza said. "Can I get you something to drink?"

"I'm fine, thanks." Matt smiled as he sat opposite Rachel.

"Can you leave us, Mum?" Rachel said, as her mother moved a cushion from the chair beside her and prepared to sit down.

"I'd rather stay, darling."

"Please, Mum."

Her mother stood up, stifled a sigh, and nodded. "I'll be just in the next room if you need me."

When they were alone, Matt turned to Rachel again. "Can you tell me about your relationship with Maggie," he began.

She shrugged one shoulder. "We've been friends since we were like, two or three. She used to be my best friend."

"Used to be? What changed?"

She shrugged again and turned her pretty amber eyes to the drizzly, grey scenery beyond the windowpane.

"Did you argue?"

Another shrug. "Not really argue."

"But there was something?"

She turned to face him. "We grew apart, that's all."

"Can you tell me why that was?"

Her eyes darted to the door, clearly concerned about her mother overhearing her. She shook her head. "No reason."

"I find that difficult to believe, Rachel. You'd been best friends for years and suddenly nothing."

Rachel's eyes welled up with tears. "I don't want to get her in trouble."

"I know you don't, but it's important you tell me anything that may affect the case."

She nodded, wiping her eyes. "Maggie started sleeping around. In fact, she was having sex with just about anybody."

That staggered Matt. He hadn't expected Rachel to say something like that about her seemingly innocent friend. Surely Maggie couldn't have changed that much since her stepfather raped her? "Are you saying she wasn't a virgin?"

Rachel laughed. "She was sleeping around! How could she have been a virgin?"

Matt shook his head. He couldn't allow this witness to stand up in court.

Rachel continued. "I feel so sorry for her. It was clearly because of her mum's illness, but she was giving us all a bad name. I didn't want to be known as a slut."

"I see." He scratched his head. "Did you see Kenny often?"

She nodded. "Every day, pretty much."

"And what did you think about him? How was the relationship between him and Maggie?"

The annoying one-shoulder shrug again. "Normal. He was nice – kind, in fact."

"So you never witnessed anything out of the ordinary where he was concerned?"

"No. Nothing. I'm sorry."

"Don't be sorry. I appreciate your honesty." He got to his feet. "That will be all, Rachel. Thank you for seeing me."

He said his goodbyes to Mrs Mendoza and walked back to his car feeling dejected.

———————

That afternoon, when Maggie called with information about the local shop owner, he sighed, more than a little relieved. Then he grabbed his jacket and keys and headed to the car.

The beautiful Indian woman greeted him with a warm smile. Her hair was tied loosely in a plait, and rolled at the nape of her neck. She was wearing an emerald green, traditional Indian sari. But it was her kindly, almond-shaped brown eyes that drew Matt to her.

"How may I help you, young man?" She smiled her warm greeting.

That threw him. On first impressions, he thought the woman was no older than his thirty years, but looking more closely, he realised she possessed an air of wisdom only borne of age.

"Hi, my name's Matthew Pierson." He handed her a business card.

Her eyebrows furrowed and she lifted her gaze back to his.

"I'm looking for Yazz."

Yazz nodded. "How may I help you?"

"My client, Maggie Simms, tells me you used to be a close friend of her mother, Emily."

Yazz nodded again. "Hang on a moment, will you?" She slid off the stool and popped her head into the room behind her.

Moments later, a middle-aged man appeared, wiping his mouth on a napkin.

"Come through, please, Mr Pierson," Yazz said, lifting the hatch on the counter.

Surprised, Matt greeted the man and hurriedly did as she asked. He followed her through to the back room which held an aroma of delicious-smelling spicy food.

She offered him a seat and sat down opposite. "Now, what would you like to know?"

Matt cleared his throat. "Is it true you were a close friend of Emily's?"

Yazz nodded. "Yes. That's correct."

"And she used to confide in you?"

Yazz looked at her hands as she contemplated her answer. "I'm only telling you this as I'm sure Emily would prefer me to help her daughter than keep her confidence."

"I understand."

"I'd known Emily all my life really, although you couldn't call us friends. My parents ran this shop before me, and Emily had lived in the same house since childhood. I was several years older than her, and had married before she started secondary school."

Matt nodded.

"One night, approximately two years ago now, I was closing the shutters around nine-thirty or so, and I heard a sound down the side of the shop. I presumed it was dogs. We'd had a spate of the bins being torn up and the contents strewn about the place. I had a pole in my hands – I use it for pulling down the shutters, you know?"

Matt nodded again. "Yes, I know the type, but I'm guessing it wasn't a dog?"

"No. I almost had a heart attack when I saw a woman slumped on the cobbles beside the wall. It was Emily."

"Emily? What had happened to her?"

"At first I thought she was drunk as I could smell alcohol. I called my husband to help me get her inside. It wasn't until we were inside, under the light, that I could see she'd been beaten, badly."

"By Kenny?"

She nodded. "She didn't tell me at first, but she eventually did. They'd been out at a wedding and, because a man had come onto her during the evening, Kenny lost his temper. He beat her up in the car and, because she was crying, he kicked her out onto the road telling her to walk home."

"The nasty…"

"And the rest. I wanted her to call the police, but she wouldn't allow me to. She said most of the police were in his debt and it would make things worse for her."

"That's terrible. Why didn't she leave him?"

"Because it was her house and she said she had no chance of getting him out."

"Would you testify to this in court?"

Yazz took a deep breath and held it for a few seconds.

"I know it's a lot to ask, but it seems the entire village doubts Maggie. She doesn't have anybody to speak up in her defence against Kenny."

Yazz nodded. "Okay. Yes, I will. I saw the state poor Emily was in that night. It broke my heart and I always felt I should have done something more to help her."

"What happened that night, after you brought her inside?"

"I bathed her face and made her a hot drink and she seemed to settle down. But then her phone rang and she rushed back outside, making me swear not to say anything. She came back the next day to apologise. And we would often catch up after that. She didn't tell anybody of our friendship, preferring to keep this place secret in case she needed to use it as a bolthole. The last time I saw her, the cancer had taken a strong hold, and she was incredibly weak. She told me she was worried about what would happen to Maggie when she died. But I made her stop talking like that, refusing to accept she was going to die. I wish I'd allowed her to tell me her concerns – I could have helped maybe?"

"Who knows? But if you'll tell a judge what you just told me, then at least you can help Emily's daughter instead."

CHAPTER 9

The heavy pelting rain made it difficult to see more than two feet in front of the car – perfect conditions for what I had in mind.

I manoeuvred into position, knowing how essential the timing was.

Her car approached, and I froze, my hands on the steering wheel. I flicked on the high beam.

As I'd expected, the car swerved as she pumped the brakes to no avail.

The car zoomed past me and smashed into and through the bollard, racing down the bank, coming to rest against a huge old tree.

This was so much better than I'd expected. I reversed, trying to see inside the car, but it was too dark. The blare of the horn though told me she was pressed up against the steering wheel. I wanted more than anything to examine my handiwork, but the sound of the crash was sure to have people rushing from their homes, I had no choice but to get out of there fast.

CHAPTER 10

The court date came around too fast. I was petrified.

Matt had explained to me that I wouldn't need to give evidence at this point. They had my statement to go on, and it was up to the judge to decide whether or not the case would need to go to trial.

Claudia drove us to the court in Manchester City Centre and, after parking as close as we could, we walked arm in arm the ten-minute hike to the main entrance. I was grateful the rain had stopped, for now at least.

Just inside the main door, we had to place all our belongings on a tray and push them through an airport-style security scanner. Then, a guard waved a large wand up and down us, one at a time. I got through fine, but the alarm sounded a couple of times for Claudia. It turned out to be her belt-buckle that was triggering the alarms.

"You need to take it off and place it on the tray, please," the guard said.

"But my trousers might fall down!" She looked at him, wide-eyed.

I stifled a giggle, but the man didn't even smile. "Put your belt on the tray and step forward."

In a huff, Claudia removed her belt and did as she was told.

She was flustered when he finally allowed her through, a few seconds later.

Matt greeted us as we stepped from the lift. "Ah, there you are. We're up next. How are you feeling, Maggie?"

I shook my head. "Sick."

He grinned. "Of course you are. Sorry – stupid question. With a bit of luck, we may be able to put it behind us today. We have a couple of great statements in your favour."

A woman approached us and it took a second before I recognised her.

"Hi, Maggie," she said. "Yvette Dawson, we met at the police station, remember?"

It suddenly dawned on me – she was the detective who had interviewed me with Donna. "Hi." I smiled. "Isn't Donna coming?"

Yvette glanced at Matt and then shook her head. "She can't make it, I'm afraid."

I felt really sick. I'd been relying on Donna and Matt to get me off, and now the lead detective hadn't even bothered to show up.

As though reading my mind, Matt patted my hand. "Don't worry. Evie is well prepared – she has all Donna's notes."

Yvette nodded and smiled. "Good luck, Maggie." She turned to Matt. "I'll see you in there." Her eyes twinkled. It was clear she fancied the pants off him.

I felt a twinge of jealousy. I don't know why. It wasn't as though Matt had been anything other than professional towards me, but I suddenly felt very territorial.

When a woman called my name, I gasped.

Matt placed his arm on my elbow and escorted us into the courtroom. My knees were knocking as I took a seat at the front of the room. I fumbled about in my pocket for my inhaler as a crushing weight in my chest prevented me breathing.

The next few minutes passed by in a whirl.

The judge and the legal teams spoke amongst themselves and sounded nothing more than a steady hum. The judge, a woman who appeared to be in her fifties, peered at me over her rimless glasses before glancing back down at the notes in front of her. Her lips were pursed tightly, making deep grooves on her top lip.

I didn't have a clue what was being said, more concerned with taking deep enough breaths in order to keep myself from flaking out in a heap in front of them all. My mouth was dry. Then Claudia hugged me and I glanced at Matt's smiling face and I presumed it must be good news.

Suddenly everybody focused their attention on a commotion taking place behind me. When I turned, I saw Kenny's sisters being escorted from the courtroom.

Claudia, still hugging me, led me outside.

"What just happened?" I asked.

"Didn't you hear? They've dropped the charges. The judge was satisfied you acted in self-defence."

My body began to tremble and I needed to find a seat. I staggered to the side of the corridor and almost collapsed into a plastic chair.

"Are you all right?" Claudia crouched beside me.

I nodded. "I... I think so."

"You're bound to be shaken up, but it's over and done with now – thank goodness."

"Hey!" Matt appeared beside us. "What a result!"

I was as shocked as everyone when tears poured from my eyes.

Claudia wrapped her arms around me as I sobbed.

When I finally glanced up, I smiled an apology at Matt, who was wringing his hands to the side of us.

Yvette Dawson strode over, a beaming smile on her face. "Great outcome. Congratulations, Maggie."

"Thanks, Evie. And thank Donna for me too, please."

The smile fell from her face and she glanced at Matt.

"What? Tell me."

Matt nodded as Claudia grasped my hands again.

"Donna was involved in a fatal car accident last night, Maggie," Evie said.

I shook my head. Donna had been so full of life. "How?"

"Nobody's certain, yet. I'm sorry," Evie said, shaking her head sadly.

The news of Donna was gutting. I couldn't get her lovely smiling face out of my mind. If it hadn't been for her, I'd have been locked up.

"Did you know about this?" I asked Claudia.

"Only since arriving this morning. We agreed to keep it from you until after the verdict. You had enough on your mind."

"Can we go home now?" I asked.

"Of course we can, duck."

We said our goodbyes, thanked Matt and Evie, then entered the lift to the ground floor.

"You okay?" Claudia asked, worriedly.

I nodded and tried to smile. "I just feel very low, right now."

"Understandable. You've been through a heck of a lot recently. At least you'll be able to put it all behind you and get on with your life."

We stepped from the court into heavy rain and stood under the overhang of the building for a few minutes.

"Doesn't look like it might stop anytime soon, we need to make a run for it," Claudia said, taking a clear plastic rain hood from her handbag and plonking it on top of her freshly set curls.

Matt bustled through the door behind us. "I'll drop you off at your car."

"Oh, thank you," she said. "We'd be like drowned rats if we had to run in this."

"Come on then? I'm only a minute or two away." Matt lifted his briefcase over his head and took off down the steps.

We followed close behind.

A few minutes later, we were all soaked and dripping on the leather upholstery of Matt's Alfa Romeo. By the time we reached our car, it had stopped raining and the sun was peeking through the clouds.

Matt pulled up and turned to face me. "I'll give you a call tomorrow, Maggie. I've had some appraisals of the house and I'll put together a few suggestions for you – if you're sure you won't be moving in yourself."

"No. I don't want to. If that's still all right with you, Claudia."

Claudia rolled her eyes. "I've told you time and time again, I would love you to stay. You, me and Sandy make a nice little family."

"Great. Then that settles it. Plus, now I've been cleared of murder, I've decided to get in touch with my old mates, starting with Rachel. School goes back in a few weeks, so I need to do it soon."

Again, a strange glance passed between Matt and Claudia.

"What now?" I shook my head. "You've been trying to get me out of the house for ages – I'd have thought you'd be pleased."

"Maybe you should just make some new friends, Maggie." Claudia patted my arm.

"Why? What's wrong with my old ones?" I asked Claudia, and when she didn't answer, I turned to Matt.

Matt shrugged. "I went to meet Rachel, to see if she'd be a witness for you."

"Okay. And what? Did she refuse?"

"No. She didn't refuse."

"Then why wasn't she at the court?"

"She wouldn't have made a good witness. She told me she

didn't believe Kenny was guilty of raping you. She said he was always polite and well-mannered whenever she saw him around you. Having her make a statement would've done more damage."

My stomach flipped and I gripped the seat on both sides of me. "Of course he was nice. He wasn't about to molest me in front of witnesses, was he?" I roared, startling even myself.

Claudia leaned forwards and rubbed my knee. "We know that, duck."

I got out of Matt's car, my mind reeling. *Why the hell would Rachel defend Kenny?* I opened Claudia's passenger door and slid onto the seat. This should have been a happy day, but any relief had been short lived.

Claudia started the engine.

She didn't say a word for a few minutes as we drove towards home.

"I didn't want to upset you. We know the truth and that's all that matters."

"Maybe *you* do, but there are plenty of others in the village more than happy to believe the worst of anybody."

"Who cares what they think? The court has found you not guilty."

"There's only one thing for it, Claudia. I'll have to move away."

Matt came around a few days later to tell me the agency had found a tenant for number eleven.

"Oh," I said, trying to absorb the idea of strangers living in my family home.

"What's wrong? Have you changed your mind?"

"No. It's just…" I couldn't put into words the emotions I felt.

"Hey. Tell me what's wrong."

"I can't afford not to, but I honestly can't bear the thought of someone living there."

"I can cancel. It's not too late?"

"Who is it? Do you know?"

"Sorry. All I know is they are coming from down south somewhere and won't be moving in for a few weeks. But they're willing to begin paying right away, and they've signed a six-month lease."

"It wouldn't be an issue if I wasn't staying here – right next door."

"I understand. You have a few days until the contract is set, so if you're not sure…?"

"It's okay. Don't tell Claudia, but I'm thinking of moving away anyway."

"Really? Where to?"

"Dunno yet. But I can't face going back to school with everyone knowing my business. I'll just get a job and find a bedsit, or something."

Matt stroked the gingery stubble on his chin. "I may be able to help."

"How?"

"I know a lovely couple in London who often take in troubled teens and help get their lives on track. Now I know you're not a troubled teen, before you pipe up, but maybe it could be a solution for you in the interim. With the money you get for the rent of next door, you'd be able to save and still go to school. What do you say? Should I give them a call?"

"Who are they?"

"My best friend Jim's parents. Agnes and Fred. You'll love them."

"All right. It won't hurt to ask, will it?"

CHAPTER 11

I watched the Asian couple close up the store. The methodical way they moved around each other was a telling sign of how many years they'd done the exact same thing, day in day out.

I chose my moment and entered through the open door and stealthily made my way to the back of the store. Bubbles of excitement fizzled in my stomach, threatening to cause me to laugh out loud.

The man locked the front door and placed the keys on a shelf beside the till before heading up the stairs. The woman's day, however, was far from over. She counted the contents of the till, placing the tray of cash in the back room. And then she spent at least another thirty minutes in there, banging pots and pans, and singing away to herself happily.

I exhaled noisily when she eventually turned out the lights. She stomped up the wooden stairs to their living area.

I stayed where I was, pressed against the end of the shelving unit at the far side of the shop, and waited a few more minutes just in case one of them reappeared.

Eventually, I took a few steps forwards, ducked under the open hatch, behind the counter and through the door leading to the staff kitchen. I was startled several times until I realised the sounds I could hear were the couple walking about above me, chattering in their own language.

I opened the door that led to the staircase and peered up, satisfied they were far enough away not to hear me. I closed the door and glanced around, my eyes settling on the oil in the pan on the stove.

"Bingo!"

I held my hand over the pan and the heat caused me to pull it away again, then I spied the triangular pastries on a cooling rack beside the sink. I picked one up and sniffed it – it smelled delicious. They were clearly what she'd been making before she finished for the day.

After inspecting the ancient stove, I pushed the pan on top of the biggest burner and ignited the gas underneath it. I grinned, feeling very pleased with myself.

As an afterthought, I shoved over a pile of boxes, jamming them behind the door that led to the stairs. Then I wedged the door, for double measure, with the pole the man had used to pull the shutters down.

Taking one final glance around, I picked up the pastry again and took a bite. Nodding my approval, I unlocked the front door and left, pulling the shutter down behind me.

CHAPTER 12

"You'll never guess what happened," Claudia said, rushing in from the street.

I trudged down the stairs, rubbing my eyes. "What? I heard the sirens in the night."

"The corner shop has burnt to the ground."

"Our corner shop?"

"Yes. They don't know how it started yet. Doreen said they took a couple of people away in an ambulance, but I'm not sure who."

I felt as though she'd body slammed me. "No! I hope Yazz is okay." I slumped down on the bottom stair, my head spinning.

"Awful business, I tell you. Doreen said she'll knock when she hears anything – she's a right old gossip that one, but she never fails to get the lowdown, I'll give her that."

A few hours later, Claudia jumped up from the sofa and rushed to answer the door.

My heart almost stopped when I heard Doreen's cockney

twang, although I couldn't make out the words. But when Claudia reappeared a few minutes later, her face told me everything.

I shook my head, feeling my eyes fill. "No, please, no," I said, tucking my legs underneath me, trying to block out what I knew was coming next.

She sighed and came to crouch beside me. "I'm sorry, duck. Seems Yazz and her husband were both inside. They were trapped in the corridor – several boxes had fallen behind the door."

I rubbed at my face and thumped at my forehead. "No! This can't be happening to me?"

"To you?" Claudia's eyebrows furrowed.

"Yeah, to me. I know it sounds crazy, but it seems anyone who is kind to me ends up dead."

"Nonsense, Maggie. It was a terrible accident, that's all. Doreen said they believe it originated from the stove. So, you see, it's nothing to do with you."

"I don't care. I've made up my mind. I'm moving to London."

"Don't be silly. Who do you know in London? And how do you intend to support yourself?"

"Matt's friends have a spare room. I'll be able to go to school there."

Claudia looked horrified as she realised this wasn't something I'd just decided. It was already planned. "You'll still need money. And who are these people? How do you know you can trust them?" She rattled off the questions like a machine gun.

Matt's found a tenant for next door. I'll be able to use the income from that to pay my way. As for the people I can stay with, Matt used to go to university with their son Jim, and he can vouch for them personally."

"Sounds like you've already made up your mind," Claudia huffed. She stomped into the kitchen and slammed around.

I'd been putting off telling her since Matt confirmed his friends had a spare room for exactly this reason – I knew she'd take it personally. But I had nothing to stay in the village for.

Especially now I knew what Rachel had been saying about me. The thought of going back to school with all my supposed friends gossiping behind my back had me reaching for my inhaler.

After a few minutes, Claudia returned with two steaming mugs of tea. She placed one beside me. I noticed her lips were still pursed.

"I'm sorry if I've upset you, Claudia. You know I've loved staying here with you, but after everything, I think it's best I put a bit of space between me and the village for a while. I'm not saying I'll be gone forever."

Her face softened and she bobbed her head. "I know, duck."

So, that was it. Two weeks later, on the twenty-fifth of August, I was on the bus heading to London and my new life.

Claudia sobbed when we hugged our goodbyes and I had a brief wobble, wondering if I was doing the right thing. But the gruff bus driver barked at us and I was on the bus with the doors shut before I had a chance to change my mind.

The trip would have been nice if it wasn't for a crazy woman who decided she would jabber away at me, without a pause, for hours. But that wasn't the worst of it, I was certain she was going to the toilet, right there on the seat. She stank.

When we pulled into the bus station, the butterflies returned to my stomach. What if I didn't get on with the couple who had willingly agreed to take me in? What if they had a set of bizarre house rules? But I was certain to discover all that very soon. I saw them through the window before they saw me. They were seated on a bench and the woman, who had a friendly face and neatly styled grey curls, helped the elderly man up from the bench. They both shuffled towards the bus.

They seemed all right, but time would tell. I fixed a smile to my face and stepped from the bus.

Agnes and Fred Bowdon seemed just as nervous as I was. They hugged me warmly and, when my case had been pulled from the bus, they led me to their shiny orange Kia.

Fred pointed out all the landmarks including the school as we whizzed by, but I didn't manage to take any of it in.

A few minutes out of the town centre, Fred pulled into the drive of a cute detached bungalow with whitewashed pebbledash walls.

I could tell the gardens were immaculately kept even though it was night-time. A cluster of gnomes filled a flowerbed beside the royal-blue front door.

Fred insisted on carrying my suitcase, but I was worried he might cark it, as, instead of using the built-in wheels, he lifted the entire thing from the boot, up the path, and into the house.

"Oh, thanks so much," I said, avoiding the use of his name. I wasn't sure what to call them. Although they'd introduced themselves by their first names earlier, I felt cheeky with them being elderly and all.

Inside, the walls were embossed paper painted brilliant white and all the furniture was highly polished wood. In the lounge, I was surprised when a girl jumped up off the sofa. She appeared a little older than me with lots of black hair, olive skin and huge brown eyes, circled with black makeup.

"You must be Maggie." She took my hand and pumped it enthusiastically.

"Erm… Yes. Hi."

"Maggie, this is Caroline. She lives here too, and you'll be going to college together," Agnes said. "I'm sure you're going to be the best of friends."

Caroline rolled her eyes cheekily at me and we both laughed. Maybe Agnes was right.

"Okay, who wants a cuppa? You must be parched, Maggie."

"That would be lovely, thanks, Mrs…"

"I'll have none of that formal how's-your-father, my name's Agnes and I want you to be comfortable and happy here. This is your home now, after all."

"Thanks, Agnes."

Fred appeared, red faced, and plonked himself down on one of the two armchairs. Judging by the contents of the side table – reading glasses, remote controls, a puzzle book, and a cup filled with pens – it was his usual chair. I made a mental note never to sit in it.

"Are you all right, Fred?" Caroline asked.

"Worn out. What the heck did you have in that case? The kitchen sink?" He grinned over at me.

"Practically. I didn't know what I'd need, so I brought as much as I could fit in. It did have wheels though."

"Hah!" He barked out a laugh. "Now you tell me."

We all set off chuckling and Agnes returned wondering what the joke was.

After drinking the tea, Agnes showed me to my room. A bigger than average single bed sat between two white bedside cabinets and a chest of four drawers was against the wall across the room. The curtains and bedding matched – white with tiny pink roses in stripes.

"Oh, it's beautiful." I hugged Agnes. "Thank you so much."

"Caroline's room is directly opposite and the bathroom you both share is just along the hallway. Our room is off the kitchen area so you should find it quite private back here."

"I don't know what to say." I looked down at my hands. "I love it."

Agnes rubbed my shoulder. "The pleasure's all ours. Matt couldn't praise you highly enough."

"Really?"

"Don't seem so surprised. Matt's a great judge of character."

Caroline popped her head around the door. "Are you settling in?"

Agnes headed for the door. "I'll leave you to it. Can I get you anything? A spot of supper?"

I shook my head. "I'm fine, thanks. Claudia made me some sandwiches for the journey."

"You know where we are if you need anything." Agnes left.

"Are you okay?" Caroline said.

I nodded, blinking away tears. "It's just so lovely here. I didn't know what to expect."

"I know, I was the same when I first arrived last year. Without Agnes and Fred I'd be on the streets. My parents died in a car accident."

"That's terrible!"

She shrugged. "Not really. They were both off their faces on smack."

"Oh. Still, it's hard to lose your parents, regardless of why."

"Yeah, I guess you're right. But this is like a dream come true for me. I wasn't exactly cared for growing up."

"That's sad. I wasn't too bad. My mum looked after me until she died of cancer." I didn't want to mention Kenny. Some things you keep to yourself.

We chatted while I unpacked my case. Caroline told me all about the college, which didn't start for another week, and all about her new boyfriend, Pierre. She made me promise not to mention anything about him to Agnes and Fred. After a while, I zipped up my empty case, and slid it underneath the bed.

"Right, I'll leave you to it." Caroline hugged me and headed off across the hall. "Goodnight, Mags."

My stomach turned. Nobody called me Mags anymore, not since Kenny. I would need to put a stop to that ASAP.

CHAPTER 13

I settled in to my new life in London with no issues. Caroline introduced me to her friends and so I was already one of the gang by the time the school term started a week later.

Caroline became the sister I never had, and I found myself telling her all about Kenny in the end. I knew she wouldn't betray me – we trusted each other.

I could honestly say I was happy. Nobody, apart from Caroline, knew anything about my past and I was treated normally for the first time in ages. Agnes and Fred, although strict, were amazing guardians. We all got on well and laughter became a daily part of my life.

One Sunday, just after dinner, I called Claudia like I did every week, to catch up on the village gossip.

"Ah, Maggie. It's so lovely to hear your voice. How's it all going?"

"Great. I love the college. It's so different to school, more laid back."

"So no regrets?" She sounded unhappy.

"I miss you, though. Tell me what's been happening."

"Oh, you know. This and that."

Surprised by her attitude, I tried a little more schmoozing. "How's Sandy? Is he looking after you?"

"His ears just pricked up. He must've heard his name."

I smiled. "Aw. So, come on. Gossip?"

"Not a lot goes on around here, as you know. But I did see Doreen yesterday. She said the shop fire was definitely caused by a pan of oil left on the cooker."

"No! She went to bed and left a pan turned on?"

"Seems so. Yazz made a batch of samosas every evening, by all accounts. She must have just overlooked it, it's easily done. The tragedy is they'd created a prison for themselves. The smoke alarms went off, but because they had boxes stacked up in the little kitchen, they were trapped behind the door leading up to the living area. Bars had been fitted to every window – they had no chance of escape."

"Poor, poor, Yazz. She must've been terrified."

"I know. Doesn't bear thinking about, does it?"

I didn't answer, lost in my own world as I thought about my mum's beautiful friend.

"I've upset you now. I didn't think. Are you all right?"

"Yeah. I'm fine. Just a little homesick, that's all."

"I know how you feel, duck. The place doesn't seem the same without you."

"I promise to come back in the next holidays, and I'll call you every week, as usual."

"Don't worry about us. We'll be here waiting when you manage to come home."

I hung up, feeling wretched. But I *had* actually missed her. And the fact she'd called her place my home made me feel like I actually belonged somewhere, which meant the world to me after everything.

CHAPTER 14

The terraced house was in darkness as I tried the front door. It didn't budge. I headed around the back and, after struggling with the bolt on the gate, wasn't surprised to find that door was also locked. I'd come prepared to break a window, but hoped it wouldn't come to that – the less mess and noise the better.

Examining the window above the sink, I realised it had a dodgy lock, and a bit of jimmying had it open in less than a minute.

It was a struggle to get up and inside, but I managed it without too much trouble.

Standing in the kitchen, I paused to take in the atmosphere.

I knew the layout of the place, and also knew the room my target slept in, but I approached with caution, just in case.

The low grumbly sound took me by surprise as I reached the top of the stairs. I'd forgotten about that scruffy little dog.

I froze at the side of the landing, as though trying to blend in with the tacky sixties wallpaper.

Then I heard shuffling steps coming from the bedroom.

"I told you to go wee-wees before we came to bed, you little rat-bag," the woman said into the darkness. "I'm going to let you sleep in the back-yard if you keep waking me up like this."

She kept grumbling until she was out on the landing and standing immediately in front of me.

"Hi, Claudia," I said.

Startled, Claudia shrieked, and took a faltering step backwards.

I shoved both hands onto her flabby chest and grinned as she crashed backwards down the stairs.

The dog launched himself at me, but I booted the little fucker down the same way his owner went.

As I slowly descended, I couldn't see the dog, but I could make out from the streetlight, that Claudia was in a bad way, if not already dead.

Feeling smug, I stepped over her and let myself out the front door.

CHAPTER 15

Caroline and I were seated at the dining table, each of us doing homework, when the phone rang. Agnes breezed in from the kitchen, wiping her hands on a towel.

"Hello-oo," she said, in her singsong phone voice. "Ah, Matt. How lovely to hear from you. Yes, dear. She's right here – two ticks."

I hadn't heard from Matt in the weeks I'd been here and my stomach flipped. I took the offered handset from Agnes and got to my feet, heading to my bedroom. "Hi, Matt."

"Hey, squirt. How's it going?"

"Fine, thanks."

"Good, good. Listen, love. I'm calling with bad news, I'm afraid."

My breathing hitched and I felt the blood rush to my face. "What's happened?"

"It's Claudia. She's had an accident."

All the air whooshed from my lungs. I grabbed the edge of the chest of drawers to steady myself. "Is she...? Is she dead?"

"No. But she's in a coma. She fell down the stairs. The police think she tripped on her dog."

"I'll get the next train. Could you pick me up at the station, Matt? I wouldn't ask, but…"

"Of course. Let me know what time you'll arrive in Manchester."

I hung up and rummaged in my school bag for my inhaler, taking two deep puffs on it. I couldn't believe it. Poor Claudia.

I found Agnes stirring a pan on the stove. She glanced up as I entered the kitchen. "What's wrong?" she asked as soon as she saw my expression.

"I've got to go back to Manchester tonight. Claudia's had a fall and is in a coma."

"How awful. Here, sit yourself down, and I'll get you a glass of water. You look pale."

"Thanks." I did feel light headed, but there was no time to waste. Claudia needed me.

"Caroline?" Agnes called.

Caroline walked into the kitchen. "Yes?"

"Go and give Fred a shout, would you. He's in his shed."

"Why? What's happened?"

"Claudia's in hospital. Can you look at train times for me, love? The bus will take too long."

Caroline rushed off and I sipped the water before getting to my feet. "I'd best pack a bag."

"I'll make you something to eat. You'll be hungry later."

We each raced around packing and grabbing stuff I might need, and got to the station within an hour. The trains to Manchester ran every twenty minutes. I hugged the three of them goodbye and promised to keep them updated.

When I was on the train, I called Matt to tell him I was due to arrive at nine-ten p.m. I felt sick every time I thought of poor Claudia, and so for a distraction, I opened up the magazine Caroline gave me. My stomach growled with the familiar hunger pangs I'd come to recognise as nerves, so I began munching on the family-sized packet of cheese 'n' onion crisps Agnes had shoved in my bag. And then I settled down for the two-hour journey.

Matt was waiting on the concourse when I arrived. His handsome face lit up and he pulled me in for a quick hug.

He smelled of soap and sunshine and I didn't want him to let me go.

"So sorry to have been the bearer of bad news, squirt. I'm hoping your presence will connect with Claudia on some level." He picked up my hand luggage, linked his free arm through mine, and led me from the station.

As we approached his car, I was surprised to find the engine running. Then I noticed there was a pretty blonde woman in the passenger seat.

Matt opened the back door and waited until I was inside, then crouched down to make his introduction. "Maggie, this is my girl-friend, Penelope."

My heart was suddenly crushed into a zillion pieces. I glared at the stuck-up bint who smiled sweetly at me, flashing her perfect teeth. I had no right to be jealous – there had never been anything between Matt and me, but I suddenly realised I really liked him.

"Where to, squirt? It's too late to take you to the hospital."

"Can you drop me off at Claudia's house, please? I have my key."

Matt swung the car around and headed towards the village. "I'll pick you up tomorrow, if you like? I have a couple of meetings in the morning, but nothing after."

"I'll get a bus," I mumbled, staring through the window. I knew I was behaving like a brat, but I couldn't help feeling he'd deceived me in some way – acting all nice, organising for me to stay with his friend's family, picking me up from the station – and all the time he had a girlfriend.

He didn't appear to notice my attitude, and continued chattering away.

"Luckily Evie told me about Claudia, or you may not have found out what had happened. She was discovered by a friend, but she'd been there a while, by all accounts – the dog had left two heaps on the carpet so it must've been a few hours."

"Poor Claudia. Who's got Sandy now?"

"I'm not sure, sorry. Maybe Claudia's neighbour?"

The only person I could think of was Doreen, but I'd find out in the morning. I couldn't go waking people up so late.

As Matt drove into my old street, I got a feeling of panic in my chest. Considering I'd lived here my whole life, I hadn't missed it at all.

He escorted me from the car and his snobby girlfriend shouted her goodbyes as though we were best mates. *Bitch!*

I nodded, and slammed the door behind me.

"You okay, squirt?" Matt asked, as he got my bag from the boot.

"I'm fine. Thanks for the lift."

"Hang on. Don't you want me to come inside with you?"

"For what? To turn on the lights? Check for bogeymen?" I took my bag from his hand. "I'll be fine, thanks. You get back to your girlfriend."

A puzzled expression clouded his face. "Have I done something to upset you?"

I shrugged. "No. I'm tired, that's all."

"Okay, I'll call you in the morning and see if you need a ride to the hospital."

I unlocked the door and entered, leaving him standing there as I slammed the door behind me. I knew I was being a total bitch, but I couldn't help myself. He was nothing but my very friendly solicitor, and yet I had clearly begun to have a crush on him. What the hell was wrong with me?

Inside, I leaned my back against the door as I breathed in the familiar scents. I squealed at a strange snuffling sound coming from somewhere by my feet. Dropping my bag, I lurched for the light switch.

Claudia's little dog looked up at me quizzically and began wagging his tail.

"Some guard dog you are." I crouched down and scratched Sandy's head. "Are you okay, boy? Mummy gave you a nasty fright, didn't she? She'll be home soon, you'll see."

CHAPTER 16

Sandy didn't seem his usual self. It was clear the poor little thing hadn't recovered from the trauma of Claudia's fall.

"Come on, boy." I ran upstairs to my room and laid my bag on the bed, with the dog right behind me. Then I headed back down to the kitchen.

Somebody had been by to fill up Sandy's bowls, but I wasn't sure when he'd had his last toilet break, so I took him outside into the back alley.

Sandy ran off into the darkness to do his business. I wasn't concerned. I knew he'd be back soon. But I was startled by a deep, throaty growl as Sandy reappeared whimpering.

"What's up, boy?" I ruffled his fur. "Oh, you silly boy what are you making all that noise for?"

The sound of footsteps approaching made me freak out, and step back towards Claudia's gate, my heart pounding. "Who's there?" I squeaked.

Whoever was approaching us, suddenly turned on a torch, illuminating black-booted feet, and dark trousers.

I grabbed Sandy's collar, and turned trying to leg it back to

Claudia's. In my panic, I'd misjudged how far I'd gone, and each gate I shoved held firmly. I turned to face the man again.

The torchlight moved upwards, showing the man wore a shirt and a dark jacket.

A familiar tightness in my chest caused me to struggle to take a normal breath and I began to wheeze. Sandy was still growling, a real guttural sound that made the hairs stand up on the back of my neck. "What do you want?" my voice was more whisper tinged with squeak. I couldn't swallow. My ears felt as though they'd filled with something hot and heavy. I froze, my eyes wide with fear.

The torchlight slowly raised, showing the man's arm, shoulder then neck. I couldn't breathe. Then, the eerie beam showed a stubbly chin, a grinning mouth and suddenly, his whole face was illuminated.

"Hi, Mags."

I let go of Sandy, and ran, frantically banging on every single gate until I reached Claudia's open one.

Sandy got there before me and ran whining to the furthest point of the backyard.

I slammed the gate behind us, but the man was too fast. He had one arm and one leg inside, and his chest was sandwiched between the gate and the brick wall.

He pushed hard against me.

My strength was no match for his. I let the gate crash back against the opposite wall, and I ran towards the kitchen door, the man close behind.

"Mags. Stop!" he shouted, then belted out a laugh. "It's me. Jake."

Jake. I froze. Stepping back from the kitchen door, I allowed it to swing open. From the light of the kitchen, I could see it was Detective Jake Stuart. Relief flooded through me and I clasped my hand to my chest. "What are you doing creeping around so late?"

"I could ask you the same, young lady."

I furiously eyeballed him, as I located my inhaler in my pocket and took two deep puffs. "I was walking the dog, for your information."

"Since when? Doreen told me nobody was staying here and I came to investigate when I saw the house lit up like a Belisha beacon."

"I just arrived back from London. I'll be staying for a while until Claudia gets home, at least."

"Yeah, nasty business that. I was one of the first on the scene after she was found. Could've sworn she'd broken her neck considering the position she was lying in."

I winced, my breathing returning to a more normal rhythm.

"You going to ask me in?"

I glanced from him and back to the dark.

"I just want to walk through to my car on the street, if that's not too much to ask?"

Reluctantly, I stepped aside and allowed him to enter. Then I called Sandy, who skulked in through the door and straight onto his bed.

"You need guard dog lessons," I hissed, then went after Jake, who had walked through to the living room.

He'd taken Claudia's carriage clock off the mantelpiece and was holding it up to the light. "Landed on your feet, didn't you, Mags."

"I haven't a clue what you're on about, but can you put that back, please." My voice sounded much braver than I felt – this man terrified me almost as much as his friend had.

"Sure, you do. I mean, a young girl – all alone in the world. You'd expect her to struggle to survive. But not you. Everything fell in your favour didn't it, Mags?" He bounced the clock on his hand.

"Can you leave now, please, Jake? My solicitor will be here soon," I lied.

"Your solicitor, eh?" Jake replaced the clock on the mantelpiece. In two strides, he stood directly in front of me, gazing down at me with a sneer on his face. "Is that how you got him to bend over backwards for you, Mags? I had wondered if he was dipping his wick."

"What are you talking about? Just go! It's been a long day."

"Maybe you should warn your fancy man to steer clear of you. He may be the next one to fall foul of Mag's curse."

"What are you trying to say? What curse?"

"How many people need to get hurt before you realise that everyone who's tried to help you since you brutally killed dear Kenny has come a cropper? Who do you think that's down to, Mags?"

I staggered backwards as though his words had assaulted me somehow. Fumbling in my pocket, I pulled out my inhaler again and took another two deep draws on it.

"Poor, Donna. She wouldn't have a wrong word said about you. And then your Indian friend, Yazz, is it? Mrs Green was lucky to escape with nothing but a cracked skull, by all accounts."

"Get out!" I screamed. "Get out – get out – get out!"

"Keep your hair on, Mags. It was just an observation." He stepped towards me again, but I'd hit the sideboard and had nowhere else to go.

He reached out and grabbed my cheeks, squeezing his fingers so hard the inside of my mouth pressed against my teeth, making my lips squish together. Then he grinned and leaned forward, kissing me full on the mouth.

I froze. A rasping sound escaped me.

"Bad case of bronchitis there, Mags. I'd get that checked out if I were you."

And with that, he was gone.

Movement slowly returned to my legs and I staggered to the closest chair and fell into it. What had he meant? Had he caused all those awful accidents? He'd practically confessed to it. But he was a policeman. He couldn't have – could he? The room was spinning. But the thought he might come back propelled me to my feet. I needed to lock up.

At the front door, I pulled both bolts across, top and bottom, and then did the same with the back door. My body was still trembling and I noticed Sandy's was too.

"Hey, boy. It's okay. Did the nasty man frighten you?" I stroked him again. "Was that who hurt your mummy?" I was still reeling from Jake's words. I picked the dog up and hugged him tightly. "You can sleep in my room tonight. What Claudia doesn't know, can't hurt her."

CHAPTER 17

I was woken by a loud hammering on the front door. Petrified, I jumped out of bed, certain Jake had come back to finish me off. But whoever it was outside had no intention of going anywhere until I answered. I figured Jake wouldn't make such a racket if he intended me harm, he wasn't that stupid.

Sandy, who had taken hours to calm down from the events of the previous night, scarpered underneath my bed. His high-pitched whine followed me downstairs.

"Who is it?" I called out.

"Doreen. Can you open up please?"

I unfastened the bolts, and the door swung in. "Hi, Doreen. Sorry, I got back last night. I came as soon as I heard about Claudia."

"You gave me a fright there, girl. I thought I'd somehow double locked the door when I came in last night. I've come to feed and walk Sandy – unless you'll take over."

"Yeah, of course I will. Come in, I'll make you a cuppa and you can tell me all about it."

We walked through to the kitchen and I filled the kettle.

"There isn't much to tell really, Maggie. I called round to bring

Claudie her Avon order. I could hear the dog whimpering behind the door, but nothing else. When I looked through the letterbox, I saw her lying there."

"Oh no. That's awful."

"It was. I honestly thought she was dead. I called the police first and then an ambulance. Luckily, our local detective was two minutes away and he came right around. He was the one who kicked the door in."

"Jake Stuart?" I tried to keep my voice light as I said his name. I poured hot water into the pot and kept my back to her.

"Yes, that's right. Lovely, he was. Ooh, if I were twenty years younger…"

I shuddered. I found the thought of anybody finding Jake attractive hard to believe.

"Anyway, we rushed inside and by the looks of her, we were certain poor Claudie was dead, but moments later, the ambulance arrived and I was blown away when they found a pulse."

I placed the teapot and two cups onto the breakfast bar. "What did Jake do?"

Doreen glanced up at me quizzically. "What do you mean, what did Jake do?"

"Oh, nothing. I just meant it must have been a shock to him if he'd thought she was dead, too." I poured the steaming tea and pushed one of the cups towards Doreen.

"Yeah. He was as shocked as me. He left soon after – he had a job to get to."

I bet he did, I thought, but I didn't let on to Doreen about my suspicions. She was such a gossip, and I had no doubt it would get back to Jake within the hour.

"I'm heading over to the hospital this morning, Doreen. I'll call in on my way back if you like, to let you know how she is."

"Would you? I was thinking about going myself, but all that air-conditioning plays havoc with my chest."

I smiled and nodded.

We chatted about nothing in particular while we finished our tea, then I got up from my stool and cleared the cups away. "I need to be making a move anyway, Doreen."

I saw her out, then went in search of Sandy, who still hadn't made an appearance. He was on my bed, dithering. He knew he was being naughty as he couldn't look at me. "You're pushing it now, mister. Claudia would have a fit if she saw you." I picked him up and carried him downstairs and out the back door.

The back gate still swung open the way I'd left it when I ran for my life the previous night. When Sandy had done his business, I secured the gate and headed back inside to feed him.

I showered, dressed and an hour later was on the bus heading for the hospital.

I queued up at the reception desk for a few minutes and was soon at the front of the line.

"How can I help you, miss?" the well-groomed man asked.

"Hi, there. I'm looking for a friend of mine, Claudia Green."

After a minute's tap-tapping at his keyboard, he smiled. "Follow the purple signs – ward one is on the first floor. You can't miss it."

As I reached the ward, I realised I'd come outside of visiting hours. Three nurses at the front desk were busy. "Excuse me," I said.

They all looked up.

"I've come to see a patient, Claudia Green. I didn't realise I needed to wait for visiting times."

"Can I ask your relationship to the patient?" the younger of the three said.

"I'm kind of her daughter."

"Kind of?"

"I live with her, when I'm not away at school. I've only just heard what happened and came right away."

That seemed to satisfy the nurse and she walked out from behind the desk.

"How much do you know about Ms Green's condition?"

"Just that she's in a coma after falling down the stairs."

"That's correct. She's suffered a terrible trauma to her head and there was a substantial brain bleed. We were a little concerned that the pressure inside her skull would be too great, but it seems to have steadied off for now."

"How bad is she?"

"I won't lie to you, miss, your friend is gravely ill. But she's holding her own and that's all we can hope for at this stage."

She stopped walking and placed her hand on a door handle. "Now, I want you to brace yourself, miss."

"Call me Maggie."

She nodded. "Your friend is connected to a machine and is being fed by a tube so don't be alarmed."

I took a deep breath and followed the nurse inside the room.

She stood to the side, and gave me a sad smile, putting her hand on my arm. "We'll be in and out to check on her, so if you have any questions, just ask."

"Can she hear us?"

She bobbed her head. "Possibly."

"How long can I stay?"

"As long as you like. We don't mind in these cases. Although we won't allow a crowd of people at once."

"There's only me." I smiled weakly. "Thanks."

I waited until she left before I glanced around. Claudia was attached to all kinds of gadgets, which made her difficult to recognise. I pulled up a chair beside the bed. "Hi, Claudia. It's me, Maggie."

I don't know what I'd expected. Even though the nurse had

said Claudia was in a deep coma, I truly thought the sound of my voice would rouse her like from a scene in a movie. Yet, she didn't react. I waffled on for the best part of an hour, but nothing.

An orderly, with a Polish accent, came in and asked if I wanted a hot drink.

I nodded gratefully.

Then, as she came back with a steaming mug, Matt suddenly appeared behind her.

"Oh, there you are," he whispered, glancing apprehensively towards Claudia.

"I told you I'd be here." I still felt pissed off he'd flaunted his girlfriend in my face.

"I've been calling you all morning."

I shrugged. "My phone's on silent."

"How is she?"

"Still out of it. Looks like crap, doesn't she?"

He nodded. "Yeah, but we're not used to seeing her without her makeup on and her hair done to perfection – she'll be okay."

"I hope you're right."

We sat in silence while I sipped my milky tea.

"Matt?" I said after a while. "How did Donna die?" I hadn't been able to shake what Jake had said to me, but I had no idea what I could do about it.

His forehead crinkled. "In a car accident. Why?"

"She crashed?"

He nodded. "Yes."

"Into another car?"

He shook his head. "No. It appears she swerved to avoid something. There were no witnesses, but she came off the road and crashed into a tree. Killed outright."

I acknowledged his words with a nod.

"What made you ask?" His eyes narrowed.

"It seems anyone I care about ends up dead or in hospital."

"Just a coincidence, squirt."

CHAPTER 18

We spent hours together, by Claudia's bedside. Several medical staff came in and out doing various tests, but there had been no change.

Just after five, Matt got to his feet and stretched. "Can I drop you off at home? I can shout you a burger, or something on the way."

My stomach growled. I nodded. "Okay. I need to get back to feed Sandy anyway – he'll be cross legged by now."

I kissed Claudia's cheek. "I'll be back in the morning, Claudia. If you can hear me, squeeze my hand."

There was no movement.

Matt put his arm around me as we walked from the room.

I left my number with the nurse at the front desk and told her to let me know of any changes, no matter how small. Then we strolled hand in hand to the car. Any onlookers could be forgiven for thinking we were an item. But in truth, he only cared for me like I was his sister.

We picked up two burger meals from the drive through and took them back to Claudia's to eat.

Sandy seemed a little better as I opened the door. He did his usual *happy to see you* dance. He wagged his tail so furiously, his entire back end wiggled from side to side. But when he set eyes on Matt, he whimpered and ran off up the stairs.

"What's wrong with him?" Matt asked.

"He's still not himself since Claudia's fall."

"Poor little fella."

"He'll soon come back down when he smells the food."

We went through to the living room.

"So, how long have you been seeing your bit of stuff?" I asked when we'd settled down on the sofa, and were munching on our food.

"Who? Penny?"

I jiggled my eyebrows.

"Two years, or so."

"Is she the one?"

He shrugged. "I guess so. We're planning to move in together as soon as we find a place."

"You'll be married with two-point-four children next."

"Is she the reason you went into a huff yesterday?"

I barked out a laugh, covering my mouth so I didn't spray him with chewed up burger. "I didn't go in a huff," I eventually said.

"What would you call it, then? You were bouncy and bubbly when I met you inside the station, and then tight lipped and flippant by the time we got to the car."

"Did she think I was rude?"

He shook his head. "No."

"Liar." I laughed and he joined in. "I was just surprised, that's all. I thought we were friends and yet that was the first I'd heard of her."

"We're friends now. But you were my client before that and there are some things you just don't discuss with clients."

"I guess. Maybe I should apologise to her."

"Not necessary. She thought you fancied me."

I splurted out another laugh. "Not likely." I could feel my cheeks redden. Had I been that obvious?

"That's good then. I can assure her she hasn't got any competition."

"As If I'd be competition for her, she's gorgeous."

"You're pretty damn gorgeous yourself, squirt."

I stopped eating and cleared my mouth. "Do you mean that?"

"Of course, I mean it. You're gonna make some man very happy one day."

I wrapped up the remnants of my food and placed it back in the bag.

"Have I offended you again?" he asked.

I gave my head a quick shake. "No. I'm tired, that's all. You'd best get off anyway, hadn't you? Penelope will be wondering where you've got to."

He glanced at his watch and whistled. "Yeah, I'd better scoot. We're supposed to be going out for a romantic dinner."

"You've just eaten an entire burger meal."

"I know. I'll have to wing it – pretend I'm just not hungry."

"Men!" I laughed, shaking my head.

"Shh! Our secret. Okay?"

"Whatever."

He bent and kissed the top of my head. "I'm going to be tied up most of the day tomorrow, but I'll call you when I'm free. Turn the bloody sound on."

"Yes, boss." I smiled, rolling my eyes at his nagging.

As I watched him drive away, I felt empty. Did I fancy him? Or was our relationship more like brother and sister? I didn't know, having been an only child. However, I knew I cared for him, a lot.

I brought Sandy downstairs and, after letting him outside for a few minutes, fed him the scraps along with his dried food. Claudia had him on a strict diet and would have a fit if she knew I'd fed him scraps – but Claudia would need to wake up and bollock me herself, wouldn't she?

I called Agnes and Fred in London to keep them updated and then, after flicking through the TV channels for a while, I tucked Sandy under my arm and headed up to bed.

During my usual nightly Facebook trawl, I was surprised to see I'd received a private message from Rachel.

> *Hey, babes.*
> *Heard you were back in*
> *town and wondered if you*
> *fancied catching up?*
> *Missed you,*
> *Rach xxx*

My heart almost missed a beat. It had been so long since we'd had any real contact, apart from the five-minute conversation in Yazz's shop. But, although I was wary of what she'd told Matt, I'd missed her too.

Oh, Rach. I'm so pleased
you contacted me. Things have
been awful between us for such a
long time. I'm sure you've heard, but
Claudia has fallen down her stairs – she's
in a coma. I would love a chance to
catch up. I've missed you so much. Xx

The message had barely sent when another popped up.

Great! How about tomorrow?
I can meet you after school –
4pm at Lardoes?
Got so much to tell you. xx

I was beaming as I snuggled down to sleep.

CHAPTER 19

I waited at the end of the street, watching the dirty fucker leave. No wonder he was so intent on getting her off with killing Kenny – he's screwing her himself!

I ducked down as he passed me and then hurriedly started the car and followed, keeping a little distance between us. He drove for around ten minutes, to a village I didn't know. Then he parked outside a pub.

He was out of the car and running across the road in front of me before I reached him. Thankfully, he didn't appear to see me.

I parked a little further up and doubled back on foot.

It was easy to spot him. I didn't even need to go inside. He sat beside the window fawning all over a stunning blonde. I wondered if Maggie knew about this.

I waited for what seemed like forever, and almost gave up, but then Matt appeared on the street, arm in arm with the woman who had a good six inches on him. They looked comical together, and I wondered what she saw in him. He was good looking, in a boyish kind of way, but didn't seem suited to her at all.

Instead of walking back to the car, they turned down the side of the pub and followed the signs for the canal.

I followed on foot. And when they'd walked for a few minutes along the bank without seeing anyone else, I pulled up my hood and jogged past them, thanking them for stepping to the side. I almost laughed out loud.

Then, a little way ahead of them, I pretended to stumble and cried out as I fell to the dirt, rocking as though in agony. I heard do-gooder Matt race towards me.

"Oh, my god, are you okay?" He dropped to my side.

I didn't waste any time. Swinging my arm around, I caught the blade in the centre of his throat.

He gripped the wound, his eyes wide and I saw a split second of recognition before he fell forward, making a grotesque gurgling sound.

His gangly girlfriend was beside us before she realised what had just happened and, as though in slow motion, she turned and began to run back the way she came.

Her long legs were only for show I found, as I caught up with her in a few strides and slammed the knife into her back.

She was strangely quiet. I'd expected at least a scream, but she fell forwards with a sickening splat – not at all graceful as her gazelle-like appearance suggested.

I didn't know if she was dead. She hadn't got a good look at me so I didn't care. However, as I stood over her watching, expectantly, she didn't move and I had a feeling I'd struck a bullseye, straight into her heart.

I took a folded cloth from the pocket of my jogging pants and, after wiping my gloved hands on it, I yanked out the knife and wrapped it in the cloth before strolling back to the car.

I was surprised at how scenic the little canal walk was, and made a mental note to come back in the summer.

CHAPTER 20

The situation with Claudia was exactly the same when I arrived the next morning. I couldn't understand how a person could just lie there for so long. I knew she had a head injury, and that she could have died – but she was in a hospital. You'd think they would've been able to fix her by now.

All day I sat by her bedside, taking a half-hour break at lunchtime to go to the canteen for some soggy fish and chips. At three thirty, I kissed Claudia's cheek, promising to return the next day.

I thought I'd have heard from Matt by then, but he had said he'd be busy all day.

The bus dropped me in the centre of the village and I strolled the few hundred metres to Larooes, a greasy spoon that was often full of kids my age. On the scruffy painted sign outside, someone had changed the first *o* to *d* with a magic marker and now everyone called the place Lardoes, which was totally fitting.

Rachel was already there, dressed in jeans and cerise pink T-shirt. Her brown suede jacket hung on the back of her chair. She jumped to her feet as I entered, and rushed towards me, her arms outstretched.

We hugged and, within minutes, we were jabbering as though we were the best of friends again. There was no mention of the months she and the rest of our friends had ignored me, and I chose not to bring it up, not yet. We caught up on everything. And, after being eyeballed by the café staff for taking up a table for so long, we ordered a bowl of chips to share and a couple of milkshakes.

Afterwards, we walked arm in arm to Claudia's so I could feed Sandy. The silly dog ran in circles in the hallway until he saw I wasn't alone and then, again, he scarpered. We found him whimpering underneath the table.

I got on all fours and laughed. "Look at the state of this guard dog."

"Aw, what's the matter, poochy?" Rachel said, crouching onto the cold floor beside me.

Sandy made a funny, whining whimper, and began licking the air, comically.

We laughed hysterically.

"Don't take it personally, Rach. He's had quite a few scares this week."

Eventually, Rachel coaxed Sandy out with the rustling of a sweet she had in her pocket. "Come on, you silly sausage."

We fed and walked Sandy along the back alley, laughing like silly kids after Sandy did a massive poo. Rachel found me gagging, as I picked up the steaming mound, highly amusing.

It felt good to laugh again. "I've missed you so much, you crazy bitch," I said.

"Me too – I'd hug you if you didn't have that stinking shit-bag in your hand."

I lifted the bag in front of me and chased her back up the alley and in through Claudia's kitchen door, with Sandy yapping at our ankles.

When inside, Rachel called home to tell them where she was. Her dad insisted on picking her up in an hour.

I didn't want her to go, but it was a school night. "Maybe you can stay over at the weekend?"

"I'd love that," she said.

While waiting for her dad, we had a coffee and sat on the sofa, Sandy sandwiched between us.

"So, I heard you'd inherited your old house?"

I nodded. "Not that I plan to live there. It seems strange."

"I'm sure it does. I was gutted to hear about your mum." She reached for my hand.

My breath hitched and I looked up at her as my eyes filled with tears.

"I'm so sorry I didn't get in touch. I couldn't cope. I've never had to deal with death before and I had no clue what to say or how to behave."

"So what changed?"

She shrugged. "My nan got sick, and the only person I wanted to call was you."

"Oh, no. Is she okay?" I'd known her nan for years – she'd taught us both to bake all sorts of goodies.

"She's been put in a nursing home. I'm ashamed to say it took something like this to make me realise how much I missed my best friend. But by then, you'd moved away."

"I wish you'd just messaged me."

"I did as soon as I heard you were back."

I nodded and wiped my tears. "I know. I hope we never lose touch again. I didn't realise how lonely I've been, until now."

"Let's make a pact. Besties forever."

I sighed. "Besties forever." We clasped our hands together.

The sound of a car horn tooting outside had us on our feet.

I stood on the doorstep and waved her off. We'd agreed she would come to stay on Friday night.

I glanced at my watch. 8.30. I was surprised Matt hadn't been in touch. I called Doreen and left a message on her answerphone, telling her there was no change. Then I sent a text to Caroline, asking her to pass the message on to Agnes and Fred. I was all talked out.

Finally, I texted Matt.

Going to bed.
Speak tomorrow – still no change
in Claudia. xx

Sandy and I were again woken by someone banging on the door.

I staggered from my bed and down the stairs, still half asleep.

Doreen looked through the letterbox as I reached the bottom of the stairs.

"Maggie, open up."

"Hold your horses. Bloody hell!" I opened the door in a temper. "What?"

She barged in and headed straight to the kitchen. "I've just heard something and I'm not certain, but I think something has happened to that friend of yours."

My legs almost gave way.

Doreen leapt forward to catch hold of me. "Oh, heck. Hang on. Let's get you to a chair."

"What happened?" I asked when I was steady again.

"I think your friend was attacked along with a woman. They are both dead, I'm sorry, Maggie."

"That's not possible. She was only here last night. Her dad picked her up to take her home."

"Who?"

"Rachel," I said, shaking my head.

"No. Sorry, love. I mean your solicitor friend. They were found last night along the side of the canal."

CHAPTER 21

I felt as though I'd been punched in the stomach. All the air whooshed from my lungs. I couldn't breathe. Doreen was in a panic, but I couldn't tell her what to do. I finally managed to scramble for my inhaler and I took several deep pulls on it.

"I'm sorry. I'm such a blabbermouth. I didn't think of the effect the news would have on you."

I nodded, concentrating on breathing in and out.

After a few minutes, I asked her to tell me all she knew.

"Dirty Derek, from Barber Street, knows someone who knows your friend's girlfriend."

"Penny?"

"Aye, that's the one. Apparently some woman was jogging along the canal and she stumbled upon two dead bodies. According to the ID found at the scene, it's this Penny and your solicitor friend. They'd been stabbed to death."

I couldn't believe it. I kept seeing Matt's smiling face when he'd left a couple of nights earlier. "Are you sure?"

She rubbed my hand and nodded. "They reckon they'd been there several hours, but because they'd gone off the normal path, and were hidden by shrubbery. It was a while before anybody found them."

"But are you sure it's him?" I couldn't believe what she was telling me.

"They haven't been formerly identified yet."

Still struggling to take enough breath, I knew I should head to the hospital for a nebulizer. I took two more puffs of my inhaler, feeling so weak. Jake's words kept running through my mind. He'd almost threatened Matt the night before Matt and his girlfriend were attacked. But he was a detective! Could he actually be capable of murder? Could it just be a coincidence that every single person who had supported me was being killed?

My initial thoughts had been for Rachel, but if my suspicions were a reality, she would most certainly be his next victim. But what could I do about it? Who would believe a well-respected police officer could be a serial killer? It sounded crazy even to me.

Doreen left as soon as she was happy I wasn't about to cark it, probably to pass her gossip on to the rest of the street.

I didn't know why I was angry with her. Without her I wouldn't have a clue what had happened to Matt. But I was so angry.

I knew I needed to tell Agnes and Fred, but decided to wait until it was confirmed.

After a short rest on the sofa, I fed and walked Sandy, before showering, and getting ready for the hospital – praying for some good news about Claudia.

I felt deflated. Although I hadn't known Matt long, he was one of my only friends, and I'd been a complete bitch to his girlfriend who also lay dead in the morgue, according to Doreen.

As I rounded the corner at the bottom of the street, a car skidded to a stop beside me.

Jake jumped out. "Just the person I'm looking for. I need you to accompany me to the station, Mags."

"What? Why?" I pushed his arm away.

He held his hands up as though backing off. "Are you resisting arrest?"

"Arrest? What the fuck are you on about? I'm not going anywhere with you." I felt sick. The thought of getting in his car made me almost pee myself again.

"We'll see about that. Stand there – don't move." He bent back into the car and I could hear him talking on the radio.

Moments later, a siren approached and a police van also skidded to a stop beside us.

"Oh, you've got to be kidding me." I shook my head, backing away from them.

Two uniformed policemen jumped out, and circled me. They read me my rights, handcuffed me, and then bundled me into the back of the van.

Trembling and alone in the back of the police van, it suddenly occurred to me what Jake had in mind – one way or another, he'd make sure I paid for killing Kenny.

At the station I was stripped and searched – my clothes were taken for forensic examination. I was given paper overalls to wear instead. Then, Jake took great pleasure in shoving me in a cell.

I cried until my face felt ugly and red. This was so unfair. They still hadn't told me about Matt and Penny, but I knew they were the people I was being accused of killing.

A few hours later, Jake appeared, an evil grin plastered on his face. "Ready to answer some questions, Mags?"

"I've told you," I growled. "Don't fucking call me that, you pig."

"Very touchy, aren't you, *Mags*? Do I need to watch myself around you? Maybe *I'll* be your next victim."

"You're such a dick."

He shoved me in the direction of the cell door. "Get a move on. I haven't got all day."

In the interview room, a female detective introduced herself to me as Julie Johnson. Her smile was kind and she reminded me of Claudia. "Are you sure you don't want a solicitor present for the interview, Maggie?" she asked.

"I don't need a solicitor. I've done nothing wrong. Will you just get it over with, please?"

"So, Mags…" Jake said.

I glared at him.

"Oops, sorry." He wiggled his face in mine. "*Maggie*." He sauntered around the table and straddled one of the chairs. "So, tell me. Where were you the day before yesterday?"

I focused on the woman and directed my answers towards her. "I was at the hospital all day."

"What time did you leave?"

"Five-ish, I guess."

"Did you go straight home?"

"No. We picked up some burgers and took them home."

"Who's we?"

"Me and Matt, my solicitor."

"Does he usually spend time with you, eating dinner and such?" Jake asked.

"No. I moved out of Manchester a few weeks ago, I was only back because Claudia had an accident." I wanted to scream that I knew all about Matt being dead and also knew who the culprit was. But how could I? And my only hope right now was to get Julie on my side.

"When did you last see him?"

"He didn't stay long. He was going to meet his girlfriend."

Jake pounced on this. "Were you jealous of her, his girlfriend?"

"Don't be so stupid. Why would I be?"

Jake shrugged. "Attractive young man, maybe you'd set your sights on him."

"There was never anything like that between us."

"You sure?"

"Why are you asking me all these questions?"

"Because, Mags, Matthew Pierson, and Penelope Judd were found dead yesterday."

I gasped. Hoping I was convincing enough. I didn't want Doreen to get into any trouble for telling me already. "What? How?"

"They were stabbed repeatedly."

Burying my head in my hands, I sobbed. "No! Who would…?"

"Exactly what we want to know. Who would want to cut their promising young lives short?"

"Why would you think it was me? I could never do anything like that."

"Really? You didn't bat an eyelid when you repeatedly stabbed your own stepfather. How many times did you sink that knife in Kenny's chest?"

I shook my head and gazed at Julie imploringly.

"No? I'll tell you, shall I? Sixty-three separate puncture wounds. Sixty-three."

Julie gasped. Right then, I knew I'd lost any chance of her support.

"That was different and you know it." Frustrated, I tore at my hair. When would this nightmare end?

Clearly thrilled his words had the desired effect, Jake grinned. "But is it though? You got away with his murder, didn't you? It's a known fact that people like you get blasé."

"People like me? What the hell are you on about?"

"You're a killer, Mags. Let's face it. Killers like you become addicted to the rush of adrenaline."

I buried my face in my hands and sobbed. A huge lump in my throat made it impossible to respond to him.

"We've got the forensic team searching your home, so you may as well come clean. They'll find the evidence, I promise you."

"That's impossible. I didn't do anything. If anyone needs to explain themselves it's you!" The words were out before I knew what I was saying.

"Why on earth would *I* have to explain myself, Mags?"

"Because you threatened Matt to me the other night. Funny that less than two days later here we are discussing his death."

Jake barked out a laugh. "I threatened him, did I?" He nodded at his colleague as if to say, *watch this*. "So what did I actually say? For the record."

"That Matt had better watch his step, having anything to do with me."

"And you took that as me *threatening* him? Not warning him to stay away from you?"

"I know what you said, but I also know what you meant and you were taunting me, telling me he'll be next."

"I don't get you, Mags. What are you trying to say?"

I was too far gone to hold back. "You planned on killing off Matt, the way you did with Donna and Yazz. You even tried to kill Claudia, but she tricked you, didn't she? She'll have you hauled off to the nick as soon as she wakes up – you'll see."

Both detectives were laughing openly as they left the room.

CHAPTER 22

It was two hours before they came back and by then I was pulling my hair out.

"Right, Mags. Where were we?" Jake said.

"I've told you – stop fucking calling me that!" I jumped to my feet and my chair fell backwards, clattering to the floor.

"Ooh!" Jake laughed. "Take a chill pill, sweetheart."

Julie rubbed my arm and lifted my chair upright again. "Have a seat, Maggie. We shouldn't be too much longer."

I did as she said.

Jake cleared his throat. "Right. You'll be pleased to discover that forensics didn't find anything of interest in your house."

"Surprise, surprise," I snapped.

"Needless to say, we may still need to talk to you again, so don't go anywhere without our knowledge, do you hear."

"Of course I hear, I'm not deaf."

He got to his feet. "Pleased to hear it. Now, Julie will arrange to have your belongings brought to you, and I will be in touch, mark my words."

Relieved beyond belief, I scowled at him as he left the room.

Julie was great. She finished her paperwork, and dropped me off at the hospital, seven hours later than first planned.

I needn't have bothered. Claudia was still in a coma and even when I blurted out everything that had happened – Matt and his girlfriend being murdered, Jake dragging me to the police station and accusing me of being the culprit – she still didn't show any signs of being aware. The longer this went on, the more I was certain she was gone for good.

Totally alone, I was able to release all the emotions from the past few days. Claudia was still alive, albeit barely, but I'd never see Matt's kind and caring face ever again. The nurses kept their distance, leaving me to wail uninterrupted, allowing me to get it all out of my system – for now at least.

After couple of hours, I figured I'd best get home to feed and walk Sandy – he'd been alone all day.

On the bus, I phoned through and ordered a pizza. As I rounded the corner of our street, the delivery van pulled up and I jogged the last few yards.

"That was good timing," I panted, handing the guy a screwed-up tenner.

He lifted his foot onto the doorstep and balanced the insulated bag on his knee while he rummaged for the change.

Sandy was yapping frantically from behind the door and, when the delivery driver had left, I opened the door. Sandy flew out, bounding about my feet excitedly.

I couldn't see any evidence of the house being searched, and I guessed Jake and his colleague had done it themselves, not a full on forensic team as he'd tried to make out.

When Sandy had calmed down, I took him out the back door for the poor pooch to relieve himself. Then, we curled up on the sofa and shared the pizza. "Don't you tell Mummy what you've been eating, okay?"

Sandy licked his lips noisily in response, and I kissed his scruffy head.

"You know what, boy? We're lucky we have each other."

After dinner, I made a call to London.

"Hello, Maggie, dear. How are you? Any improvement with Claudia?"

"I'm fine thanks, Agnes. And no, no improvement at all."

She sighed. "What did the doctors say? Is this normal?"

"I guess so. They don't seem concerned. But, listen, Agnes, I need to tell you something. Is Fred around?"

"Yes. He's right here. What's wrong?"

I took a deep breath before continuing. "It's Matt and his girl-friend. Agnes, they were found dead yesterday. Somebody killed them."

"I'm sorry, Maggie..."

Muffled voices followed and then Fred came on the line. "Maggie, love. I'm going to have to call you back."

Hearing the devastation in their voices caused my own tears to flow. Up until then, I'd been numb, had been since the day my mother died. I sat back down with Sandy and sobbed. For Matt, for my mum, for Claudia – in fact for everyone, including myself.

Although I detested Jake, the more I thought about it, I knew I must be way off the mark. He was shocked when I accused him earlier. And although he could have kept me locked up for a few days without pressing charges, he hadn't actually kept me any longer than necessary. I still detested him, of course. But I was confused.

I roared and tore at my hair.

Sandy shot off the sofa and headed for the kitchen.

I roared again, and punched and punched the cushion as tears mixed with snot. I felt so tired of trying to keep my shit together. Was I lashing out at Jake because I didn't want to believe the alternative – that I *was* actually jinxed? Since Mum had died, things had gone from bad to worse. Most girls my age have never had anything to do with death, but not me. I felt so alone.

After a while, my tears dried and I went in search of Sandy. I found him trembling in his basket underneath the kitchen table. "Come on, boy. Let's go out for a quick walk and then it's bed time."

Sandy stared at me warily before venturing from his bed.

As we stepped outside, I noticed the sky had turned a murky grey colour and it was threatening to rain. I opened the gate and let Sandy go out alone while I ran back indoors to fetch my jacket. When I returned, Sandy had disappeared.

I went up the cobbled alley. It wasn't dusk yet, but the clouds were casting shadows in the doorways. "Sandy!" I called. "Come on, boy."

Several dogs began barking from behind closed gates as I passed. I expected to find Sandy behind one of the wheelie bins dotted along the alley, but as I reached the end with no sign of him, my heart sank.

"Sandy!" I gave a long high-pitched whistle. "Come on, boy."

Nothing.

A thought struck me. Sandy had probably followed me back inside when I went for my jacket. I exhaled noisily and shook my head. "Bloody idiot," I grumbled as I set off at a jog.

"Sandy? Come on lazy pooch," I called as I reached the back door. "I wasn't the one who needed exercising, thanks very much." I stopped abruptly, and stared at the empty basket.

CHAPTER 23

After searching the house, I ran back out into the alley in a panic. Where the hell could he be? I'd only left him alone for a minute, if that. But, although the light was fading by the minute, Sandy was nowhere.

I ran back through the house and along the street to Doreen's, and hammered my knuckles on her white uPVC door.

Doreen immediately appeared behind the glass. She dramatically placed her hand on her chest when she saw it was just me making all the racket.

"Maggie! Calm down. Whatever's the matter?"

"It's Sandy. He's gone."

She grabbed her beige jacket that hung over the banister. "What do you mean, gone?" Joining me outside on the doorstep, she turned and locked the door.

"I took him out for a walk and he ran off. One minute he was there, the next – he'd just vanished."

"He's probably got the scent of a bitch in heat. He did that to Claudie once and the dirty little rascal stayed out all night. He'll be back, you'll see."

We set off walking up and down all the surrounding streets

and alleyways, but there was no sign of Sandy. I knew Doreen was probably right, but, after my luck lately, feeling of doom settled in the pit of my stomach.

As we walked, I updated her on Claudia. I omitted to tell her I'd spent most of the day in a cell, and, surprisingly, her informants hadn't told her either.

After an hour of trudging around, we arrived back at Doreen's front door.

"Thanks, Doreen. I'll let you know if he shows up by morning."

Walking a few more steps up the street, I was horrified to realise I'd left both the front and back doors wide open. I walked inside, holding my breath.

My heart thudded as I scanned each room. No Sandy.

I ventured out to the dark alley again, and called him once more. I hated being out there in the dark and an odd sound made me run back inside.

I slammed the door and double locked it behind me.

"Silly dog. If you do decide to come home in the early hours you're locked out there until morning," I muttered as I slid the two bolts into place.

I couldn't sleep. Alternating between worrying about Sandy not coming back? How I would tell Claudia I'd lost her dog? And grieving for Matt. Lovely, gentle, and caring Matt. It was hard to believe I'd never see his crooked grin ever again.

At two-thirty, I trudged downstairs and unlocked the door again, certain I'd see the little mongrel curled up on the doorstep, highly embarrassed by his behaviour. But no. He wasn't there. If I had a car I'd drive the streets. A couple of nights earlier I'd have been able to call Matt, certain he'd drop everything to assist. But now, besides Rachel, who also didn't have a car, I had nobody to turn to.

Warming a mug of milk in the microwave, I headed back up to bed. I finally managed to get a couple of hours' sleep, but the dreams kept coming. I dreamed of a coffin with the lid partially lifted. Barely breathing, I approached it, the sound of my heart-beat thundering in my ears. I reached out, my fingertips touching the cool wood.

I paused.

Braced myself.

Pushed the lid away from me.

A cry caught in my throat as the wasted, cancer-ravaged face of my mum appeared. I wanted to run as far away as possible, but something forced me to stay. I pushed the lid further needing to see her, all of her, one last time. I'd missed her so much. The lid wouldn't move any more. It had snagged on something and I couldn't quite get to her.

"Mum! I need you, Mummy. I can't bear my life without you. Please." I pushed with all my might. The lid wouldn't budge, not one inch. I was aware I was dreaming, but it was the first time I'd dreamed of her since she'd died and I wanted to see her one last time. I was petrified of forgetting what she looked like.

I noticed a long piece of wood, the length of a baseball bat only slimmer, lying on the carpeted floor beside the table. I grabbed it, shoving it into the opening, and used my weight to prise the lid off.

It suddenly shifted and clattered to the floor on the other side of the coffin. Surprised I'd actually shifted it, I almost followed it.

Righting myself, I turned, desperate to see my lovely mother for one last time. But the image before me had changed.

Kenny sat up in the coffin and grinned at me, but it was the limp and bloody dog he held towards me that almost killed me.

I screamed and screamed. Suddenly back in my room, I tried to calm my thundering heart. "What the fuck?"

Launching myself from the bed, I raced downstairs and out the back door, desperate to see the little pooch. But the yard was still empty.

I couldn't shake the image of Kenny grinning, but I kept repeating to myself it was just a dream. It didn't take a psychologist to explain the reason behind it – Kenny was to blame for everything, including the missing dog. Maybe not directly, but if he hadn't raped me, then how many of the following events would have happened? I guessed none of them.

I checked the wall clock and sighed. It was only five a.m. yet there was no point going back to bed. I did a load of washing and ran the vacuum around the place instead, in the hope Claudia would be home soon.

After showering, I headed out to walk around the streets and alleyways again, although I knew in my heart it was pointless. Whatever had happened to Sandy I had no doubt in my mind he was gone for good.

"Still no joy?" Doreen's voice interrupted my gloomy daydream as I turned back onto our street.

"Oh, sorry, Doreen. I was miles away. But no, he hasn't come back yet."

She shook her head and rolled her eyes. "Are you off to the hospital?"

"I was going to, but how can I? What if he turns up?"

"Don't worry. I can keep an eye out for him and I'll let him back in."

"Would you? Okay, then. If you don't mind, I *will* go to visit Claudia."

"Give her a big kiss from me. Tell her to hurry up and get better – I miss her."

"Will do, thanks, Doreen."

CHAPTER 24

I spent the day at Claudia's bedside, urging her to wake up. But nothing. Not a flicker.

As I came back from the toilet mid-afternoon, I caught the tail end of a conversation between Claudia's doctor and his colleague.

The doctor smiled and made for the door.

"Hang on," I said. "What's happening?"

The doctor glanced back around as though I was a pile of rubbish. "Are you a relative of Mrs Green?"

"I'm kind of her daughter. We live together and she cares for me."

He nodded. "We have just examined Mrs Green and are happy with her progress."

"What progress? She hasn't made any."

"I know it may seem like that to you, but I can assure you, after the extensive trauma she received, I'm confident we should see some results in the next week or two."

I sat down. "Week or two? Are you sure this is normal?"

"Perfectly normal, miss. I'll be back around tomorrow if you have any further questions."

I sat in silence for another hour or so. I'd run out of things to say, there was only so much one-sided waffle one person was capable of. I jumped when my phone vibrated in my pocket. I walked out to the corridor.

"Hello?"

"Hi, Maggie, it's me," Rachel said brightly.

"Oh, hi, Rach. How are you?"

"I'm okay. Where are you? I'm about to leave home."

"Leave home?"

"Yes. I'm supposed to be staying at yours tonight – did you forget?"

I gasped. "I'm so sorry. I've had such a shit week. Maybe you'd be better off leaving it for tonight – I'm not the best of company right now."

"You poor thing. Is Claudia all right?"

"Still the same."

"I'll bring something for dinner, and you can tell me all about it. What do you fancy?"

"Anything. But are you sure?" I put a smile in my voice, grateful for a friend. But suddenly a pang of guilt gripped me. Was I putting Rachel in danger?

"Positive. Will you be back by six? I'll ask Daddy to drop me off."

I glanced at my watch – 5.15. "Yeah, should be. I'll go and catch a bus now."

I said my goodbyes to Claudia and headed off to the bus stop.

I hadn't heard from Doreen, so I didn't know if Sandy had shown up yet, or not. I prayed he had.

I arrived home just before six. Rachel and her dad were parked in the street, waiting for me.

She jumped out and her dad helped her with her bags. He

nodded towards me, his face not breaking his sour expression, then he got back into the car and drove away.

"Was it something I said?" I asked.

Rachel laughed and hugged me. "Oh, don't mind him. He's a worry wart."

"What's he worrying about?"

She shrugged and grinned. "Truth?"

I nodded.

"He's worried about me spending time with a killer."

Startled, I looked up at her. "Really?"

She laughed. "Don't worry about it – he's just being silly."

"But I do worry. That's why I had to move away. People don't seem to care what Kenny was doing to me – I had no choice."

I opened the door and waited for Sandy to come bounding towards me. But he didn't.

"What is it?" Rachel asked.

"Sandy ran off last night and he hasn't come back yet. I was hoping Doreen had found him and brought him home."

"Oh, no. Poor little fella. I hope he's all right."

"Me too."

We carried her stuff inside, leaving her overnight bag on the bottom tread of the stairs and the shopping bags in the kitchen. Then I opened the back door and scanned the empty yard.

"Sandy!" I called. "Come on, boy." When he didn't appear I closed the door. "I'm going to see if Doreen has him. Do you want to come?"

Rachel shook her head. "I'll unpack this lot, if that's all right, and then start cooking." It was a dream of Rachel's to open her own restaurant one day. Although her mum wasn't good in the kitchen, her nan had been fantastic, and she'd taught her how to cook from an early age.

"I won't be long and then I'll help you, I promise." I knew going to Doreen's was a pointless exercise, but the little mutt had been on my mind all day. Claudia would be devastated if she knew I'd lost him.

Doreen shook her head as she opened her door. "Still nothing?"

"I was hoping he was in here with you."

"Sorry, love. I was in and out all day, but there's been no sign of him."

"Maybe I should ring around the dog's homes. He may have been picked up."

Doreen shrugged. "Maybe. But he's been chipped so I'm sure they'd have contacted you by now."

I exhaled noisily. "I haven't a clue what to do next, then. I hope he gets back before Claudia comes to."

"How is she?"

"No change," I said, sadly.

"Not looking good, is it?"

"Nope. Not at all."

CHAPTER 25

I found Rachel chopping mushrooms and onions in the kitchen.

"Still not turned up?" she asked.

I shook my head. "It's as though he's vanished. Now, what can I do to help?"

"Oh, nothing, it's all sorted. I'm doing spag bol – is that all right?"

"Perfect."

"There's a bottle of Coke in the fridge, if you want some?"

I grabbed a couple of beakers from the cupboard and poured us both a drink. When I placed a glass in front of Rachel, I noticed her eyeing me suspiciously.

"What?" I asked.

"You seem different. Is there something you're not telling me?"

"I've had a week from hell, Rach."

"Because of the dog?" She balanced the wooden spoon against the pan handle and turned to lean her back against the worktop.

As I tried to tell her what had happened, tears welled up and spilled from my eyes and down my cheeks. I hadn't expected to cry. It was all I seemed to do lately.

"Hey! Come here." She pulled me into her arms and held me tight.

After a few minutes, I backed away and snagged a piece of kitchen roll from the holder on the wall.

"So, what happened?"

"My solicitor, Matt Pierson, was killed."

She gasped. "The one who came to my house?"

"Yeah."

"How?"

I shook my head. "Stabbed, I think. Fucking Jake Stuart is trying to pin it on me."

She screwed up her face in disbelief. "You're kidding, right?"

"I wish I was. He's been a total shit since Kenny... you know?"

She nodded. "They were best friends, weren't they? I'd hate Jake as an enemy. I can imagine he'd be a real dick."

"Thank God you see him for what he is – everyone else seems to love him."

"I've never liked him. He gives me the willies." She shuddered, and turned to stir the contents of the pan again.

I considered telling her the rest, but decided not to. We were only just getting back on track and I didn't want her to think I was crazy.

"So why would he think you killed Matt?"

"I dunno. I think he just wants to punish me. He's fuming because, in his eyes, I got away with killing Kenny."

"But they mustn't really think you did it, otherwise you'd be arrested, surely." She reached for her glass and sipped the Coke.

"They did arrest me, yesterday."

She gasped, spilling the Coke down her lemon-coloured T-shirt. "Really?"

"Yeah. They dragged me off to the station and took my clothing for forensic testing."

"Fuck! Maggie, why didn't you tell me?"

"I'm telling you now."

"You know what I mean. The cops suspect you of killing a guy – I'd be going out of my mind."

"I am. Believe me. And it's not just Matt who was killed. He was with his girlfriend. They're both dead."

I could tell by her face, she was having difficulty processing this, so I chose not to mention Yazz and Donna.

"I need to use the loo. Won't be a sec," she said, her smile was unconvincing.

I nodded and sighed. I'd misjudged her, and I wouldn't be surprised if she suddenly remembered a prior engagement.

A bubbling sound from the pan had me on my feet. I pulled the food off the flame and lifted the lid. The delicious smelling tomato sauce resembled molten lava.

"Oh, shit. Did it stick?" Rachel said, suddenly behind me again.

"No. I think it's all right." I grinned.

"I haven't even boiled the water for the pasta."

"No problem, I can do it if you've got to go."

"Go where?" She wrinkled her nose.

"I just thought…"

"Shut up! I'm going nowhere. I know you didn't hurt anyone, Maggie. Did you think I did?"

I nodded. "It's got to be a shock for you – it was for me and I was certain of my innocence."

"*I'm* certain of your innocence, silly. Now shift while I finish the dinner, I'm starving."

After we'd eaten, we shared the washing up. Then Rachel produced some cheesecake she'd been defrosting in the fridge.

"You're joking, aren't you? I'm stuffed.

"That's fine – it'll keep until later."

Here we were, acting like regular teens – something I hadn't been able to do for months.

"Will you come for a walk with me?" I asked. "I need to buy

milk and bread for breakfast and I've got to keep looking for Sandy."

"I'll need to borrow a coat. I forgot to bring mine."

"I should have something in my room, if not Claudia has heaps of cardigans."

"I'm not wearing an old woman's cardigan! I'd rather freeze."

I laughed at her horrified expression.

"Come on upstairs. I'm sure I have something you can wear."

A few minutes later, we headed off to the corner shop. Yazz's had been our nearest but there was another a couple of streets in the opposite direction.

"So tell me. What happened to your nan?" I asked as we walked.

"She was getting confused and became a danger to herself. You know how fab she used to be in the kitchen?"

I nodded.

"She kept leaving stuff on the stove top – she almost burnt her house down a couple of times. Luckily Mum called in the last time or Nan would have gone up in smoke."

"Shit. Does she mind being in a home?"

"She did at first. In fact, she made Mum's life a misery. I actually thought she should have come to stay with us, but Mum was scared she'd kill us in our beds. But now, Nan seems settled and has made a couple of friends. She's much happier."

"Oh, that's good."

Rachel waited outside the shop while I popped inside and then we walked home via the back alley.

Rachel gave a piercing whistle using her thumb and forefinger.

"Shit, Rach," I said. "You almost deafened me."

She grinned.

We passed Claudia's back gate and walked to the far end of the alley before retracing our steps.

"Can we get in the back way?" Rachel asked.

"Yeah, I didn't lock the gate just in case the little bugger came back."

I pushed the gate open and followed her through as I rooted in my pocket for the keys.

Rachel abruptly stopped walking, making me to bump into her.

I stepped around her and turned to see what she was pointing at. I screamed and threw myself down beside Sandy's bloody and broken body.

CHAPTER 26

"He's dead! Oh my god, he's dead," I sobbed, lifting the matted, bloody mess into my arms. "Get the keys, Rach. Open the door."

I looked up at Rachel who was frozen to the spot, her hands pressed to her mouth.

"Rachel!"

She suddenly reached for the keys and fumbled at the lock before the door swung inwards. She stepped inside and turned on the kitchen light.

Following her inside, I lay Sandy down on the kitchen floor tiles and, with tears streaming down my face, I examined the poor little dog. "I think he's been stabbed."

Rachel crouched down beside me, also close to tears. "Who would do this?"

"Some crazy bastard, that's for sure." I closed my eyes, trying to shut out the vision of Jake's face swimming before my eyes.

I rushed to my feet and threw up in the sink.

Rachel rushed to my side and rubbed my back. Her face had lost all its colour and she looked as though she was about to flake out.

"Go and sit down, Rach. I'd better tell Doreen what's happened and then I'll have to find something to put the poor little fella in – we can't leave him there."

Out on the street, I puffed on my inhaler and I leaned against the front wall while I took several deep breaths. *Why the hell was this happening to me?* Sandy had been the sweetest little dog. He didn't have a bad bone in his body – unlike the rotten bastard who'd done this to him.

After a few minutes, I walked to Doreen's house and tapped on the door.

"Is it good news?" she asked, a grin on her face, as she appeared before me.

"I'm sorry?"

"Sandy? Isn't that why you're here?"

"Oh." I rubbed my forehead then burst into tears.

"My dear. Whatever's happened?"

"Sandy did show up," I sobbed, "he's... he's dead."

"What?" She grabbed her jacket from the banister again and slammed the door behind her.

Back at Claudia's, Doreen found an empty box underneath the stairs and we placed Sandy's limp and broken body inside it.

"What happened to him – he's cut to ribbons," she said.

"It looks as though he's been stabbed," I said then gritted my teeth. A raging hatred for the person responsible boiled my blood.

"Stabbed? Who'd do such a thing? We need to call the police."

"I've already called them," Rachel said.

'What did you do that for?" I snapped.

They both turned to stare at me.

"Sorry, but I'm sick of the sight of the police. They'll probably accuse me of doing it."

"No they won't." Doreen shook her head. "Why on earth would *you* want to do such a thing to this poor wee mite?"

"I wouldn't, but that won't stop them trying to pin it on me."

"They won't," Rachel said. "And anyway, I'm a witness. We looked outside when we first got here and he definitely wasn't there then."

"What time was that?" Doreen asked.

I looked at my watch, trying to work my way back from 8.45. "Six-ish."

"Then what did you do?"

"I made dinner," Rachel said. "We sat in the kitchen for an hour or so, and then we went through to the lounge for a while before heading out to the shop."

Doreen glanced at her phone. "So that only leaves a ninety-minute window. You'd have heard somebody coming in the yard if you'd been in the kitchen."

"That's true," I said.

"Leave it with me." Doreen marched off towards the front door.

"What you gonna do?" I called after her.

"I'm going door knocking. Somebody must have seen something." She rushed from the house.

"I'll make you a coffee?" Rachel got to her feet and filled the kettle.

I stared at the box in the middle of the kitchen. "What am I supposed to do with him? We don't even have a garden to bury him in."

Rachel shook her head. "See what the police say. But my nan's cat died a while ago and somebody collected him from the house and took him to be cremated. She had his ashes on her mantelpiece in a lovely little box. Maybe you can do that for Claudia?"

I nodded.

We took the coffee mugs through to the lounge where we both sat on the sofa.

"I'm so glad you're here, Rach. I couldn't stand being alone right now. But, honestly, I'm scared I'm putting you in danger."

"What you on about?"

"I haven't told you everything." My voice cracked, I didn't want to tell her, but what choice did I have? "Since my mum and Kenny died, it seems anybody who shows me any kindness…" I sniffed.

"Claudia was just an accident – you said so yourself. She tripped over Sandy."

I shook my head. "It's not just Claudia and Matt. Detective Donna Sullivan drove off the road and hit a tree the night before my court appearance. She stood up to Jake Stuart and told him to back off me. And then Yazz, the shop owner, died in a fire just a week after giving a statement that helped the judge find me innocent."

"That was a freak accident. I read it in the paper. They said the fire caused a stack of boxes to fall and wedge behind the door, trapping them inside."

"Quite a coincidence though, don't you think?"

She shrugged.

"Then Claudia fell and was left for dead. Matt and his girlfriend were stabbed to death and now poor Sandy. I think it would be safer for you if you call your dad to pick you up."

She gripped my hand in hers. "I'm not going anywhere."

"You do believe me, though?"

"Well…" Rachel reached for her cup and sipped at the contents before continuing. "I really think you're working yourself up over nothing."

"I wouldn't call Sandy being stabbed to death nothing, Rach." I jumped to my feet and stomped back through to the kitchen. The box made me stop. I picked it up and slid it into the cupboard under the stairs until I could work out what to do with it.

A knock at the door startled me.

Rachel came into the hall ahead of me and smiled an apology. "I'll get it."

I nodded and returned to the sofa.

"Hello, Rachel. What are you doing here?"

My heart pounded at the sound of Jake's voice.

"I'm friends with Maggie."

"Of course. I forgot about that. I'm responding to a report made this evening about a dog."

"Yes. I made the call. Come on in."

My stomach was in free-fall as I heard her show him through to the lounge.

CHAPTER 27

I reached for my inhaler as Jake entered the room and took two deep pulls on it.

"Hey, *Mags*." His eyes glistened spitefully.

I shook my head, and forced myself to ignore his taunts.

"So, tell me – what's the problem?"

"Claudia's dog went missing last night and turned up tonight, dead. I think he's been stabbed."

Jake's eyebrows lifted. "Stabbed?"

"Yes," Rachel said. "We found him on the back step and he has several deep gashes all over his body."

A smirk played at the corners of Jake's mouth. "Another one bites the dust."

I jumped to my feet. All the hatred I'd been holding in burst out. "What the fuck's that supposed to mean?" I screamed.

"Whoa!" Jake stepped backwards and raised his elbow to ward me off.

"Maggie!" Rachel said, stepping in between us. "Calm down."

"Rachel, don't you see what he's trying to do?"

Jake held his hands up and shrugged at Rachel, as though to *say 'What the hell have I done?'*

"Please, take a seat, Detective." Rachel indicated the chair opposite and then pulled me down beside her on the sofa.

I snatched my arm from her grip and turned to glare at Jake. "This is pointless. You may as well just go, Jake. We have nothing to report – it was a false alarm."

Jake curled his top lip. "So there's no dead dog?"

"Just go!"

"Maggie!" Rachel hissed. "Yes. There's a dead dog. He's in a box under the stairs."

"And who do you suspect has done it? Let me guess. Me, by any chance?" Jake said.

Confused, Rachel turned to me, and back to Jake. "Of course we don't think it was you."

"*You* may not, sweetheart, but your little mate does – don't you, *Mags?*"

I wanted to tear his laughing eyes out of his smirking fucking face. If he didn't go soon, there was no telling what I'd do to him. "Just go, Jake. I don't want to speak to you." I turned to Rachel. "This is why I didn't want you to call the police. I knew he'd come. What better way to get away with murder than to investigate it yourself."

Rachel gasped, blinking uncontrollably.

Jake laughed. "Oh, this is classic. Hasn't Maggie told you what she thinks?"

Rachel shook her head. "I don't know what you're talking about."

"Tell her," he said to me. "Nope? Okay, I'll tell her myself. It seems your crazy little friend thinks I'm responsible for the deaths of four people and assault of Claudia and now, I suspect, the death of the yappy mutt."

Rachel turned to look at me, clearly waiting for me to deny it, but I raised one eyebrow instead and continued to stare at him, defiantly.

"Hang on. You mean you really think *he's* responsible?"

"It's no more unbelievable than me being responsible."

Jake blew a raspberry. "Oh, I think it is, young lady. I'm a respectable member of the community unlike you. Daddy killer."

Rachel cried out and jumped to her feet. "I think you should go, Detective."

Jake's face creased in a smirk, making my blood boil.

"You heard her," I spat. "Get out and don't come back."

He cocked an eyebrow at me. "What about the dog? Don't you want me to take some notes?"

"I want you to get out of this house right now. I mean it. Go!"

He shrugged and then left.

When I heard the door close behind him, I began to shake.

"Oh, Maggie. Come here." Rachel pulled me into her arms. "Oh my god, you're terrified."

"Do you see why I didn't want to call the police? I knew he'd come. He has it in for me, Rach."

Her expression altered for a second.

"What?"

"Nothing."

"Just tell me. What are you thinking?"

She sighed. "I see he's a dick but do you really think he's responsible for everything else?"

"I dunno. I can't think of anyone else who'd want to harm people connected to me. Can you?"

"Not really. But I don't think it could be him either. Couldn't it just be a string of coincidences?"

"So, you think Sandy just tripped and fell on a knife? Picked himself up and fell again and again, and then dragged his mutilated body onto the step for maximum effect?"

"Don't be stupid. Of course I don't. But the other deaths could be coincidental."

"So you keep saying." I stormed through to the kitchen where I bolted the back door and filled the kettle.

"I'm so sorry," Rachel said, appearing behind me.

I took a deep breath and exhaled noisily. "I know how crazy it sounds, which is why I didn't tell you earlier. I just hope Claudia can recall what happened when she wakes up."

The sound of banging through the wall startled me.

"Is somebody living there now?"

"I s'pose so. Matt organised an agency to rent it out. The last I heard was that a couple wanted it, but couldn't move in right away. They paid six months in advance to hold it."

"Why would anybody do that? You'd just wait until you were ready to move, wouldn't you?"

"That's what I thought, but Matt didn't think it was strange. Apparently it's difficult to find a house to rent in the village."

"Interesting. I'll tell my mum. She's been wondering what to do with Nan's bungalow. She doesn't want to sell it in the hope Nan gets better."

"What are the chances of that?" I asked.

"Zero. But there's no convincing Mum of that. Maybe if she rents it out first, it may give her enough distance to finally let it go."

"It couldn't hurt. Matt used the agency on Stockport Road. I wonder who's living next door. It seems weird to have strangers living there."

"Did you manage to clear it all out?"

"It's being rented furnished. I got out my stuff and also the things of my mum's I wanted to keep. Matt arranged for the rest to be removed." I sighed.

"You miss him, don't you?"

I nodded. "I didn't know him that well, I guess. But he was really good to me. Which reminds me, I'd better call Agnes and Fred tomorrow – she was devastated when I told her he'd been killed."

Rachel rubbed my arm and smiled sadly.

Feeling my bottom lip quiver again, I braced myself and nodded at the kettle. "Fancy a hot drink?"

"I'd rather have a vodka."

I burst out laughing. "Good luck with that. Claudia's teetotal."

Rachel rolled her eyes dramatically. "Do you have any drinking chocolate then?"

I opened the cupboard above the kettle and forced my emotions away. "Horlicks? Will that do?"

"Perfect. Do you fancy a slice of cheesecake to go with it?"

My stomach lurched, but I couldn't ruin it for her. "Yeah, why not?"

We took our cups and plates through to the lounge and slumped on the sofa.

I tried to act normal, but all I really wanted to do was cry. I didn't want Rachel to see that side of me – I kept thinking about her walking away when I needed her the most.

CHAPTER 28

"You awake, Maggie?" Rachel said, standing over my bed.

I groaned. "What time is it?"

"Just after nine. I've brought you a cuppa."

I forced myself to a sitting position and took the mug. "Thanks."

"Did you get much sleep? I heard you up in the night."

"I haven't a clue, but it feels as though I've only just closed my eyes – I'm shattered."

"I didn't know if you planned to go to the hospital, but I called my mum and got the details of the pet crematorium. They'll send somebody over this afternoon to pick Sandy up."

"Oh, thanks, Rach. I hadn't planned on going to the hospital. I'll just call them and see if there is any change. Do you have plans?"

She shook her head. I thought I'd just hang around here again today. We could watch a movie this afternoon, if you like?"

"Are you sure? Please don't feel as though you've got to stay."

She shook her head. "I don't. I told my parents I'd be here for the weekend. If that's all right with you?"

"Of course, it is. I'll just drink this and have a quick shower in case they arrive early."

While I was in the bathroom, I could hear a female voice singing in the bathroom next door. My stomach flipped. I didn't think it would bother me to have strangers living in my ex-family home, but I hadn't planned to be living right next door when I initially made the decision to rent it out.

I tidied myself up and met Rachel in the kitchen.

"There isn't much in the fridge that's edible," she said, closing the fridge door.

"I haven't really been eating at home. We could go and grab some goodies when Sandy has been collected, if you like?"

"Sounds fab. I might just have a slice of cheesecake while we wait. I'm starving."

I laughed. "Cheesecake? For breakfast?"

"Yeah! What's wrong with that?"

I shook my head. "Nothing at all. Go for it." I could have barfed in the sink at the thought of eating cheesecake. It had been hard enough to stomach the night before. "I'll make another cuppa, I think, and maybe a slice of toast."

"You have toast, I'll have yummy cheesecake. Deal?"

"Deal."

The doorbell rang.

"Shall I get it?" Rachel asked, heading to the door.

I braced myself and nodded.

As I buttered a slice of toast, Rachel came back in. I turned and noticed a dark-haired man hovering uncomfortably in the hallway.

"He's here for Sandy, Maggie."

I put the knife down and wiped my hands on a tea towel.

"Hi. He's in here." I shuddered as I opened the cupboard door and pointed at the box.

"I need to get some details first," the man said.

"Oh, of course. Come on through." I led him into the lounge.

When we'd filled out the forms, he picked up the box containing Sandy and with a heavy heart, I watched him load the little fella into his van.

Back inside, Rachel held her arms open and drew me into them. "You okay?" she whispered.

I nodded, swallowing back a huge lump in my throat. Knowing if I began to sob, she would run for the hills. I felt guilty for thinking this way, but it's what she'd done to me when I needed her once before and I naturally had my guard up.

"So what do you wanna do for the rest of the day?" she asked.

"I need to call the hospital and probably Agnes too, and then I'm free to do anything you like."

"I know you're not in the mood to go traipsing around the Arndale Centre, so how about we go to the supermarket and grab some more goodies and come back here? We could have a pamper day."

"That sounds great. Are you sure you don't mind staying in? I know you love mooching around the shops on a Saturday, but I feel like a real wet blanket at the moment."

"Only for something to do. But I'm more than happy to hang out here."

I sighed. "Oh, good."

"You've had so much to handle lately. Plus, I'm desperately in need of a facial."

"You're not kidding!" I shoved her arm playfully.

"I'll go and tidy the bedroom while you make those calls, if you like?"

"Cheers. Five minutes and I'm all yours."

The ward sister told me there was nothing to report on Claudia, but promised me she'd call if anything changed. I hung up and dialled the Bowdons' number. Caroline answered.

"Hi, matey. How's it going?"

"Maggie, hi! I've been thinking about you for days. Fred told me about Matt. Are you okay?"

"Oh, you know – coping, I guess. I don't know when I'm gonna make it back."

"We'll be over there on Thursday – did Agnes tell you?"

"No. What for?"

"The funeral. I think we're staying in a hotel."

"There's no need. We have plenty of room here."

"What about Claudia?"

"It's unlikely she'll be home, there's still no change there. But even if she is, Agnes and Fred can have my room and we can doss down on the sofa."

"Okay. I'll tell them when they come home. They're in town at the moment. I can't wait to visit you, I've missed your ugly mug."

"Charming. I've missed your ugly mug more."

We laughed and she filled me in on everything that had been happening in school, before hanging up.

"I'm ready when you are, Rach!" I called up the stairs.

Rachel came trudging downstairs. "Oh, I meant to tell you, I saw the mystery neighbour earlier."

"Did you? Who is it?"

"Some woman. She seemed friendly enough. She said, hi."

"Oh, good. I should call in later and introduce myself, I guess."

I watched as she laughed and squealed with that girl as though she didn't have a care in the world. I'd soon put a stop to that.

The bitch had ruined my plans – taken what was rightfully mine, and I intended to make her pay.

Rachel and I spent the rest of the day pampering ourselves. Using what we found in the bathroom cupboard, we gave each other a facial, followed by a manicure and a pedicure. Rachel painted her nails fluorescent purple and mine ruby red.

It felt good to do something mindless and girly for a change, although the ache of sadness was never far away. By the time we hurried arm in arm to the chip shop, Rachel and I were back to how we used to be.

The phone was ringing as we arrived home so I hurried inside, certain it would be the hospital with news of Claudia. The sound of Agnes' soft voice brought tears to my eyes.

"Hi, Maggie. Caroline said you'd called earlier."

"Yeah. I just wanted to see how you were."

"I'm fine. Sorry to go all loopy on you the other day, but the news of Matt floored me."

"I know. I shouldn't have blurted it out like that."

"There was no other way to do it."

"Caroline mentioned you were coming to the funeral. Did she tell you I said you can stay here?"

"She did, but I'd rather not, if that's all right. Fred gets tetchy staying at someone else's house. We'll be better in a hotel."

"Are you sure? Caroline is welcome to stay here with me, in fact, I'd love it."

"I'm sure she'd love that, too. The funeral is at eleven a.m. on Thursday, so we'll arrive in Manchester on Wednesday. I'll get Caroline to text you with a time."

"Aww, I'm excited. And I'm so looking forward to seeing you all, though I wish it could be for a different reason."

"I know, love, me too. Now tell me, how's Claudia?"

"Still no change. I'm beginning to think she'll never come round."

"She will. The human body is miraculous. All the time she's lying there, she will be healing."

"I know you're right. Anyway, I'll let you go. See you Wednesday, Agnes."

"Can't wait."

I found Rachel in the kitchen plating up the fish and chips.

"I hope you don't mind," she said, already stuffing chips in her mouth. "I'm starving."

"Of course I don't mind – dive in. It was just Agnes, returning my call."

"What's she like?"

"Ah, she's lovely. Although I wasn't with them long, I really feel as though we're close. Caroline too, it was as though I finally had a sister."

She handed me a plate. "Aren't we like sisters?"

"Yum, thanks. Yeah, but it's different to live with someone. Caroline was a pain in the backside – we would get on each other's nerves and bicker, but it was good to spend time with her."

We took our plates and the ketchup bottle through to the lounge and both sat on the sofa.

"I couldn't imagine having to go and live with another family. You're so brave."

"Hardly brave – more a case of having to, than wanting to." I tucked into my fish ravenously.

"Yeah. But you are brave. I could never have done what you did."

I stopped eating and wiped my mouth. "I think you would've, if pushed."

"Do you want to talk about it?"

I felt my chest tighten as my mind drifted back to that night. "I'd rather not."

"Was it really that bad?"

"What do you think? I killed the evil bastard, didn't I?" I shoved my plate onto the coffee table, no longer hungry.

"Aw, I'm sorry, Maggie. I wasn't trying to upset you. It's such a massive thing to have to deal with alone and I just want you to know I'm here for you if you want to talk about it."

I nodded. "I know that and I do appreciate it, but it's all just too raw at the moment."

After dinner we settled down on the sofa to watch some Saturday night TV. Doreen popped in during the evening to say none of the neighbours had seen anybody hanging about the night before. This came as no real surprise.

CHAPTER 29

Rachel's dad tooted his car horn on Sunday afternoon.

"Come home with me," Rachel said. "Mum will have made a yummy roast and Dad can always drop you back again later."

I'd never really got along with her parents. They made me feel like scum, the way they looked me up and down. They were never nasty to my face, but Rachel had let it slip that they would prefer her to be friends with *Samey Amy*, a snooty kid who lived just up the road from Rachel, whose parents were obviously loaded.

"No, it's fine. Thanks anyway, but I need to visit Claudia and you'll need to get ready for school."

"Do you want me to come back later? I could go to school from here."

I laughed, as I picked up one of her bags. "I can imagine your mum's reaction if you told her that."

"I'm seventeen, not seven," she snapped.

"All right, keep your hair on!"

"Sorry," she giggled, crossing her legs as though she wanted to pee. "But so long as I go to school what difference will it make? I just don't want to leave you alone after everything that's been happening."

146 | NETTA NEWBOUND

"I'll be fine, honestly. I'll be at the hospital most of the day and I'll probably have an early night – I hardly slept with you hogging the duvet the past two nights." I opened the door and stepped out onto the street.

"Cheeky bitch!" she hissed, swatting at my arm.

Stifling a grin, I wiggled my eyebrows, desperate to make her believe that I wasn't actually petrified of spending the night alone without even Sandy for company.

Rachel's dad jumped from the car and opened the boot.

"Hi, Mr Mendoza," I said.

"Maggie," he said, with no eye contact.

Rachel hugged me and made the shape of a phone with her finger and thumb as if to say, *call me*.

I nodded and waved them off.

Two Healthcare Assistants were changing Claudia's sheets when I arrived at the hospital.

"Oh, sorry, miss. We're running a little late today – staff cuts."

The way they lifted and threw her about reminded me of the butchers handling a slab of meat.

"Hey, be careful." I rushed to Claudia's side.

"It's okay, she can't feel it," the younger of the two said.

"That's not the point – just be a bit nicer or I'll complain."

I noticed an angry look flash between them as they continued the job in hand.

They left soon after.

"Idiots," I said, shoving the door closed behind them.

I pulled the chair up beside Claudia and told her all the news. I considered not breaking the news about Sandy, but figured it was good practice for when I had to tell her for real. When I ran out of things to say, I rummaged through a pile of magazines I'd found in the day room and chose the newest ones, which were still over three years old, and I read aloud until the light changed and I could no longer see the words.

Reluctantly dragging myself to my feet, I kissed Claudia on the cheek. "I'm off now, Claudia, but I'll be back first thing in the morning," I whispered.

I was so tired. If I thought I'd get away with it, I'd curl up on the armchair and stay the night, but I knew the nurses wouldn't allow that. I headed to the bus stop.

When home, I made some toast and trudged upstairs for an early night. After what felt like hours, I reached for my phone and logged into Facebook. Claudia must've disconnected the internet after I left for London and I didn't have much data on my phone so I hadn't been online for a few days. I was surprised by a series of alerts.

My stomach flipped to see I'd been tagged in several posts – it reminded me of the last time this had happened and all the nasty messages I'd received from my so-called mates. Taking a deep breath, I braced myself and tapped on the most recent message.

'Wonderful weekend with my bestie. So glad you're back in town, Maggie.'

My cheeks grew hot and tears pricked my eyes. I was grateful and relieved for her kind words. I checked the rest of the messages and they were equally lovely. It was such a nice feeling, knowing I was no longer alone in the world, but I wouldn't allow my guard down just yet.

I lay back down, feeling hopeful. She was all I had left from my past and I needed her more than I cared to admit.

The next few days flew by and on Wednesday, I left the hospital early to buy some groceries ready for Caroline coming to stay.

Claudia was still the same and I could tell by the doctor's face that he was also a little confused why she wasn't responding the way they predicted.

Loaded down with shopping bags, I slammed the taxi door shut and fumbled in my pocket for my door key.

The cab drove away and another vehicle pulled into the vacant space.

I glanced behind me and my insides dropped to the pavement.

"Oh, for fuck's sake," I said under my breath and braced myself for a fight as one of Kenny's crazy sisters stepped from the car.

"Hello, Maggie," the woman sneered.

"Listen, I'm really not in the mood. Just leave."

"Leave? Now why on earth would I do that?"

"Because you're not welcome around here, that's why."

"Tough. I live here." She stormed past me and let herself into number eleven.

Gobsmacked, I stared at her retreating back and then at the firmly closed front door.

CHAPTER 30

I couldn't believe it.

All this time, Kenny's sister had been living next door and it suddenly all made sense. This woman and her nasty sister had warned me at the court that they'd make me pay, and, it seemed, they hadn't just been spouting hot air like Claudia had insisted.

Stunned, I picked up my bags that had somehow landed on the ground at my feet. I headed inside. I didn't know what to do. I would have reached out to Donna, or Matt, a few weeks ago, but it seemed she'd taken all my support structure away one by one.

Another thought struck me. She'd seen Rachel at the weekend, so she would know I had another friend. What if she tried to get to her? Reaching for my phone, I called Rachel and exhaled loudly when she answered.

"Are you okay, Maggie?"

"I am now, Rach. I just had an awful thought."

"What about? About me?"

"That woman you saw at number eleven…"

"Yeah, what about her?"

"She's only one of Kenny's nasty sisters."

Rachel gasped. "Has she done anything to you?"

"No, not really. But I think I may be wrong about Jake Stuart. I think she could be the one who's terrorizing me."

"I'll be right over." The phone went dead in my ear.

Rachel was banging on the front door half an hour later.

I let her in and she glanced at the pile of groceries still lying where I'd dropped them in the hall.

"I forgot about that lot. I'll have to put it all away before Caroline arrives."

"Caroline? Oh, your friend from London?"

I nodded. "Yeah, it's Matt's funeral tomorrow."

"Of course. So what are you going to do about the bitch next door?"

"What can I do?"

"It's your house! You can kick her out to start with."

"I don't know if it will be that easy – she signed a twelve-month lease."

"So you can't force her to move out?"

"I won't know until tomorrow – the rental agency will be closed now."

"Call the police, then. Even dick'ead Jake will have to admit this is a strange coincidence."

"I'm not calling him. No way do I want to see his smarmy face around here again – he puts the wind up me."

"What if I asked my dad to be here? Jake wouldn't be horrible to you with an adult around."

I considered her suggestion, but I wasn't keen. Her dad didn't like me. "I'll have a think about it. Come on, give me a hand to put this lot away and I'll make us a nice cuppa."

Ten minutes later we were back in the lounge, two mugs of instant latte cooling on the coffee table.

"So, you think this woman may be responsible for killing Sandy?"

"Not just Sandy. I think she's done away with everyone I care about in order to repay me for killing her brother."

"Really? Then you defo need to call the cops. It might be you she turns on next." Rachel patted my knee.

"Or you."

She gasped. "Is that what the phone call was about? You were checking I was still alive?"

"I know I sound like a paranoid schizo, but I'm flipping petrified she'll get to you – you're the only person I've got left."

Rachel hitched herself up on the sofa beside me and wrapped her arm around my shoulders, pulling my head tight against hers. "I don't think you're a schizo, but I do think we need to tell someone. If you're right, God knows what she'll do next."

"Okay, I'll call the agency tomorrow and see if I have any way of evicting her and then, when the funeral's out the way, I'll call the police station. But I would prefer it if your dad was here. Do you think he'll mind?" I figured any adult was better than nobody.

"Not if he thinks I might be in danger – you know what he and Mum are like with anything to do with me."

"Yeah, but this will make them hate me more, I bet you."

"Who cares? And anyway, they don't hate you – they're just over protective of me."

"So, when you tell them that someone is attacking and killing anyone I'm close to, how do you think they'll react?"

Rachel's eyes widened. "Oh, shit! When you put it like that…"

We laughed our arses off.

"Maybe I'll ask him not to tell my mum, or she'll have me locked up."

"Good plan."

Someone knocked at the door and I jumped. I grasped hold of Rachel's hand, my heart racing.

"It's okay. Won't it be your friend?"

I breathed out, trying hard to calm myself down. I got to my feet and took several deep breaths before heading to the front door.

Caroline launched herself at me as soon as I appeared on the doorstep.

"Whoa!" I laughed as she spun me around, squealing and fussing over me.

"It's so good to see you."

"Aw, you too, Caz." I was touched by how excited she seemed. We'd been friends, of course, but I wasn't sure if she actually liked me or if she'd just put up with me for the sake of a quiet life seeing as we lived together.

When we had settled down, I hugged Agnes and Fred, who were standing beside the car each holding one of Caroline's bags.

"Hi, are you coming in for a bit?"

"We won't, if you don't mind. We need to find the hotel and then we're meeting up with James a little later to discuss the details for tomorrow. Shall we pick you both up on the way to the crematorium in the morning?"

"Please. What time?"

"The service is at ten-thirty, but we will need to find it, so say, nine, nine-thirty to give us plenty of time?"

"Perfect, we'll be ready."

We waved them off before I showed Caroline inside.

CHAPTER 31

"Hi." Rachel jumped to her feet as we entered the lounge.

"Rachel, meet Caroline. Caroline, this is Rachel, the friend I told you all about."

Caroline nodded, ignoring Rachel's offered hand.

"I'll leave you to it. You must have a lot of catching up to do." Rachel picked up her jacket from the back of the chair.

"Don't be silly. Why don't you stay for tea?"

"I called my dad, and he's on his way. Nice to meet you though, Caroline."

Surprised by the frosty energy passing between them, I walked Rachel out to the street.

"Are you okay?" I whispered.

She nodded. "Yeah, of course. I've got heaps of homework to do. You're lucky."

"That's all right then. I'll text you tomorrow when I've heard from the agent." I cocked my head to number eleven.

"Don't forget." She set off walking down the street.

"Hey, where are you going? Your dad's not here yet."

"I told him I'd start walking. Don't worry. He'll only be a few minutes."

A feeling of dread settled in my stomach. "Come back in, Rach. I don't like the thought of you walking; it's almost dark."

"Go on in," she hissed, over her shoulder. "I'll be fine."

I watched until she turned the corner before reluctantly going back inside.

"She seems nice," Caroline said as I entered.

"Liar." I grinned. "It was obvious you didn't like her."

"Oops. And there was I thinking I'd pulled it off."

I laughed. "Just don't take up acting."

"I was surprised to see her here after everything you told me about her. The way she gave you the flick when you needed her the most."

"Yeah, I know. She's apologised for that though."

Caroline looked at me over the top of her glasses. "That's okay, then."

"Shut up, you sarky cow." I shoved her and we both set off giggling again.

"Nah, seriously, Caz. She's gutted for treating me so badly and I've been grateful for her friendship – you won't believe what's been going on around here."

"Spill?" She kicked off her shoes and curled her feet underneath her bottom.

I shook my head. "I don't want to go into it now – can we wait until after tea?"

"Tea? I don't drink tea."

"Dinner. You know what I mean." I rolled my eyes and shook my head.

She grinned. "What are we 'avin' fer tea?" she asked, in the worst Mancunian accent I'd ever heard.

It used to annoy me when she took the mick out of me, but this time it made me feel warm and fuzzy. I hadn't realised how much I'd missed her. "Erm, shall we have some eggs and kippers, or do you fancy apples and pears?"

She could hardly breathe for laughing, which caused me to join in.

"It wasn't that funny!" I said between pants.

"It was. You just said we'd have slippers and stairs for dinner in cockney rhyming slang!"

The tears rolled down my cheeks and I struggled to breathe. It felt so good to laugh. Properly laugh.

"Come on, let's make *dinner*," I said, when we'd calmed down. "I've bought all the ingredients for tacos – I know that's your favourite."

"Ooh, yummy."

Standing in the small backyard, I could watch everything that bitch and her silly friend were doing. I was less than six feet away from them and yet they didn't have a clue I was there.

It annoyed me how relaxed they seemed. Maggie deserved all she had coming to her.

I hoiked up a ball of phlegm and spat it at the window.

They both stopped giggling for a second as they turned to see what had caused the soft tap, then they turned back to face each other and continued with their incessant chatter.

CHAPTER 32

"Do you know where the Manchester Crematorium is?" Agnes asked as we climbed into the back of their rental car.

I winced. "I've been, but apart from a general direction, I don't remember how to get there."

"Never mind. We have this gadget, but we can't get it working." She indicated a sat nav on the dash.

"Oh, I can work it. Give it here."

Within a couple of seconds, we were headed towards Chorlton-cum-Hardy, an area on the opposite side of Manchester.

Agnes filled us in on the details her son, James, had given her. "The police think Matt and his girlfriend must have stumbled on a druggie. Apparently the canal they were walking alongside is notorious for it."

"For what? Murder?"

"No. For drug deals and muggings and stuff."

"So they don't have any suspects?"

"Apparently not."

It surprised me the police hadn't told Matt's family I was a suspect. I hadn't told anybody except Rachel, but I'd expected it to all come out. I hadn't told Caroline yet, but I promised I'd fill her in after the funeral. It bothered me that Jake hadn't let me know I was off the hook – the last I heard was that I shouldn't leave the area.

My heart hammered as we pulled into the crematorium car park. I hadn't expected to recognise it. I'd been in such a daze on the day of my mother's funeral. I wanted to turn and run.

Caroline seemed to pick up on my fear. She linked her arm through mine and gave me an encouraging smile.

As we approached the front of the beautiful old chapel, the palpitations in my chest were becoming difficult to disguise. I was taking long deep breaths and felt incredibly light headed. "I can't go in," I whispered to Caroline, unhooking her hand from my elbow.

"We'll follow you in, Agnes," Caroline called. "Save our seats."

Agnes turned, her eyebrows furrowed. "Are you okay, Maggie?"

I nodded. "I'm fine. You go in."

Caroline led me back towards the car park, stopping at a wooden bench.

"You go in, Caz. I don't want you to miss it."

"I'm fine out here. I didn't really know him anyway. I only came to support you."

"Really? Oh, that's so sweet."

"Hey, I don't do sweet." She nudged my ribs with her elbow. "Are you trying to ruin my street cred?"

"You're a twit."

"That's more like it."

We sat on the bench, quietly watching hordes of people heading into the chapel. Not surprisingly, I didn't recognise any of them.

"Was this where your mum was cremated?"

I nodded. "I didn't think it would bother me, but I just can't face going in there."

"We can hold our own service for him, if you like?"

"How?"

"Wait there."

Caroline headed off towards the chapel, returning after a few seconds, holding two long-stemmed yellow roses.

"Come with me." She handed me one of the roses, and pulled me up with her free hand.

We walked down the side of the chapel, into the beautiful gardens at the rear. I noticed several benches with donation plaques.

We stopped just off the path underneath a stunning willow tree. Its sweeping canopy of yellow leaves bent and stretched, teasing the ground like a golden waterfall. We stepped underneath the wispy shelter.

"Is this okay?" Caroline asked.

"It's lovely. But what should we do?"

She shrugged. "I dunno, maybe say a prayer? Or say what he meant to you and goodbye? It doesn't have to be out loud."

I nodded. "Okay."

"I'll go first and then I'll leave you alone." She stepped forward and closed her eyes. Then, after a minute or so, she saluted and placed her rose on the grass beside the tree trunk.

I waited until she was out of earshot before I fell to my knees. I hadn't a clue what to say. "I feel so stupid talking to a tree, but I guess you'd find that hysterical." Tears filled my eyes and I tried to blink them away. "I'm sorry I couldn't face going into the chapel, but I really want you to know, if you're listening, how much I appreciate all you did for me. You were the most selfless person I've ever known and, without you, I don't know where I'd have ended up." I placed the rose beside Caroline's. "Goodbye, my sweet friend. I'll miss you." Deep sobs took over my body and I was powerless to stop them.

After a few minutes, I was aware of Caroline pulling me into her arms. We sat huddled together on the grass.

"I hope you haven't snotted all over my jacket," Caroline said, after a few minutes of silence.

I smiled and wiped my eyes. "We'd better get back. They'll probably be finishing soon."

She got to her feet and helped me up. "Come on then. Do you feel better now?"

"Much better. Thanks so much, Caz."

As we rounded the front of the chapel, the doors opened and people emerged from the building. We stood to the side and waited for Agnes and Fred, who appeared a few minutes later with a handsome dark-haired man, who had red-rimmed eyes.

The man ruffled Caroline's hair and extended his hand to me. "Hi, I'm Jim. You must be Maggie. I've heard a lot about you."

"Me too. I mean I've heard a lot about you, not about me." I stumbled over my words and felt myself blush. Jim was Agnes' and Fred's son and they'd often talked about him.

He winked. "I know what you meant. Do you fancy a drink? We're all heading ten minutes down the road to the wake."

I nodded.

"We'll follow you, James," Agnes said. "Don't go too fast, mind, we don't know this area like you do."

CHAPTER 33

As we piled back into the hire car, my phone buzzed in my pocket. It was a text from Rachel asking if I'd called the agency.

Sorry, Rach. Didn't have time. Will call them as soon as I get a minute.

I'll come over after school.

Ok

I should have made time to call the agency earlier, but I'd refused to let Caroline know what was going on. I had enough to contend with without her rabbiting down my ear about everything as well.

While having a glass of lemonade, I mingled with the other mourners, but I didn't know anybody. One woman asked how I knew Matt and I stuttered something about being a friend, rather than saying he was my solicitor. I was relieved when the buffet was opened and the woman scurried off in search of a vol au vent or two.

I slipped out of the side door and sat on a chair at the entrance while I called the rental agency.

The phone was answered by a cheerful-sounding receptionist, and when I told her who I was she put me through to a man.

"Kelvyn Wightman speaking. How may I help you?"

"Hi, Kelvyn. My name's Margaret Simms. I own a property you have on your books – eleven Junction Road."

"Ah, yes. What can I do for you, Miss Simms?"

"I have an issue with the tenants. Is there any way I can have them move out?"

He cleared his throat. "Erm, not without making a whole lot of trouble for yourself. A twelve-month lease has been signed and unless the tenants have violated the terms of the lease, then it's pretty difficult, to be honest. Can I ask you what they've been doing?"

"They haven't actually *done* anything. But I've just discovered they are the sisters of my abusive stepfather and I really don't want them living in my family home."

"I'm sorry, Miss Simms, but unless they either stop paying the rent, use the property for anything illegal, or violate the terms of the lease, I'm afraid you're pretty much stuck with them."

I buried my head in my hands when I hung up. Of course that would be the case – they'd have made sure they were safe and secure before letting me know they were living there. They wouldn't take any chances of being kicked out.

I messaged Rachel.

Agency said I'm stuck
   with them for 12 months

FFS! So there's
nothing you can do?

Not a thing. Did you ask your
dad to join us later?

Yes. He'll be there.

Ok. Message you
when I get home.

I headed back inside and found Caroline sitting with Agnes and Fred. They all had plates full of food in front of them.

"Oh, here she is," Agnes said, placing her plate on the table. "Do you want Fred to get you something to eat, love?"

I shook my head and slid into the booth. "I'm not hungry, thanks."

Agnes put her arm around my shoulders. "We've just been talking. The weather's meant to pack in tomorrow so we're thinking of leaving tonight."

"Oh, really?" I glanced at Caroline, who was clearly as disappointed as me.

"Never mind," Fred said. "I'm sure Claudia will be out of hospital soon and you'll be able to get back to school."

"Yeah. I hope so."

We stayed for a little while longer. Jim and a few of his and Matt's mates told a few hilarious stories, highlighting the side of Matt I'd never known. Although I laughed along with the rest of them, I felt a crushing emptiness every time I thought about his crooked smile and twinkly brown eyes. I jumped to my feet as soon as Agnes made the suggestion of getting on the road.

We did a detour to their hotel to collect their belongings. Then they dropped me off at number thirteen.

"Are you coming in for a cuppa while Caroline gets her things together?"

They glanced at each other and Fred nodded. "That would be lovely. We'd need to be quick, mind."

I showed them through to the lounge while Caroline ran upstairs for her bag.

Caroline reappeared and, leaving her things by the front door, she came into the kitchen where I was busily making the tea.

She closed the door leading to the hallway. "You didn't get to tell me what's been happening. You promised."

"There's no way I can tell you now – it'll take too long. I'll call you tomorrow night and tell you all about it."

She squinted at me as though she thought I was just fobbing her off.

"I swear, Caz, I'll call. So long as you promise not to tell Agnes. She'd only worry."

"Are you sure you're all right? I don't like the thought of leaving you alone if something's happening that would make Agnes worry."

"I'm fine. And anyway, I'm hoping it'll all be over by tomorrow." I picked up two mugs and nodded at the other two on the worktop. "Grab them for me, will you?" I went back into the lounge with Caroline close behind me.

Twenty minutes later I was alone again. Tears had pricked my eyes as I hugged them all goodbye on the doorstep, but I rapidly blinked them away for fear of Agnes noticing.

As I turned back to the house, I saw the curtain twitch in number eleven. I scowled and stomped inside.

CHAPTER 34

I watched as the bitch and her visitors said their goodbyes. It would have been an emotional scene if I gave a flying fuck. She waved at the car until it turned the corner and then headed back through the front door.

I tidied the cups away and my phone buzzed.

Are you home yet?

Sorry, Rach. Yes, I am.

Will come to yours soon.
Dad will meet us there when
he finishes work.

Cool, see you soon x

I washed up the cups and tidied away the previous night's dishes from the draining board. I was walking back into the living room as there was a knock at the front door.

I could hear raised voices, one of them Rachel's, and my stomach dropped. I ran to open the door.

I was startled to see Rachel and Kenny's two sisters standing on the pavement.

"Go on, get inside with your snivelling mate," the older of the sisters snarled at Rachel, raising her arm as though she was about to strike her.

"You fuck off back where you belong, you fat bitch," Rachel retaliated, turning on the woman like a Rottweiler.

"Just ignore her, Rach. Don't stoop to her level." I grabbed my friend's arm and dragged her inside, slamming the door behind us.

"What the hell was that all about?"

"They started it," she spat. "Nasty pair of bitches have picked on the wrong person."

"Okay, okay. Calm down. What time's your dad getting here?"

She took several deep breaths and glanced at her watch. "He shouldn't be too long."

"Should I call the police then?"

"No. Dad said it's best if we go to the station. That way we'll probably get somebody other than Jake."

"Did you tell him?"

"I told him the bare minimum. No point him stressing until he has to."

A series of bangs sounded from next door and I gaped at Rachel. "What the hell are they doing in there? I hope the police believe me this time. Maybe there's some way they can get me out of the lease."

"If they're being abusive like they were just now, then surely they can't expect to stay. Even if they don't believe all the other stuff, I'm witness to their aggression."

"I hope you're right."

A car horn tooted outside and Rachel ran to the window. "It's Dad. Are you ready?"

I felt sick. "No."

"Come on, you'll be fine. You have me and Dad in your corner."

I winced. "You at least."

She grabbed my arm and led me from the house.

Rachel got in the front seat and me in the back.

"Hi, Mister Mendoza." I smiled.

He nodded and indicated to pull away. "Now, I guess you should tell me what's been happening."

"I told you, Dad," Rachel cut in, flashing her father a disapproving glance. "Somebody has been doing horrid things to Maggie and we just found out it could be the new tenants at number eleven."

"I'd rather Margaret tell me the unedited version herself please, Rachel."

I cleared my throat, preparing to explain everything from the beginning.

"No, Dad. She's already shitting herself. You'll hear every detail when she tells the cops. Please don't make her have to do it twice."

He sighed and shrugged. "Watch your language, young lady."

Nobody said a word for the rest of the fifteen-minute journey.

We didn't go to the small station closest to us as it was rarely manned and was Jake's nearest base, so we went to the larger one in the city instead.

Inside the cold, intimidating building, we approached the uniformed officer at the desk.

The officer didn't make eye contact with me, choosing to acknowledge Rachel's dad instead.

"What can I do for you, sir?"

Mr Mendoza cleared his throat. "Can we speak to somebody about an issue with a neighbour?"

I quickly turned to look at him. I would have opened with, *I want to report a murder*. Yeah, a little over dramatic, but I wanted them to take me seriously.

"Certainly, sir. Can I take a few details?"

"My name is Franklin Mendoza, but the complaint is regarding Margaret Simms." He pointed to me.

The officer nodded. "Take a seat and I'll get somebody out to you shortly."

We sat in silence for the next ten minutes. A young, dark-haired detective appeared and introduced himself as DC Duncan Jones. He ushered us through to a teeny grey room.

"So, maybe you can tell me the reason you're here. All I've been told is that you are having an issue with your neighbour."

"It's a lot more complicated than that," I said, unsure where to begin and feeling self-conscious with Rachel's dad being there.

"Maybe, if you give me a brief summary so I know which page you're on."

I nodded. "Basically, I was arrested for killing my stepdad a few months ago."

That caught his attention. "Go on."

Tears sprang to my eyes and I glanced at Mr Mendoza before continuing.

"Kenny, my stepfather, raped me on the day of my mother's funeral, and made it clear that he intended to make it a regular thing. I had no choice – I needed to stop him in some way."

"So, was this reported at the time?" The officer appeared confused.

"Oh, yes. It went to court and everything. The judge agreed it was self-defence."

"I see."

"The thing is, the night before the court appearance, the detective in charge of my case died. She was run off the road in her car."

The detective tapped his pen on his lips.

"Then, a woman who was a witness for me died in a fire."

"Okay. I really don't know where you're heading with this, but—"

"I know it sounds all over the place, but I need to tell you from the beginning, Detective. Please listen to me."

He tossed the pen to the table and leaned back in his seat – nodding for me to continue.

"My solicitor arranged for my family home to be rented out and I went to a new school in London. While I was away, Claudia Green, my next-door neighbour, the woman who had taken me in, was found in a coma after falling down the stairs. I came back to be here for her, but since I got back, Matt Pierson, my solicitor, and his girlfriend were stabbed to death."

"So, we have three dead bodies and one person in a coma. Are you going to tell me you know who's responsible?"

I nodded. "Since I've been back, somebody took Claudia's dog and left him on the back doorstep, stabbed to death."

Mr Mendoza jumped to his feet. "What the...? Rachel, you didn't tell me all this. You said she was having issues with her neighbour and Jake Stuart."

"And you are?"

"I'm Frank Mendoza, Rachel's dad. Rachel and Margaret are friends."

The officer turned back to me. "Can I ask you why you didn't report any of this before now?"

"I tried to. I called the local station and they sent Detective Jake Stuart who made out that I was the killer. You see, he was a friend of Kenny's, my stepdad, and he's angry I hadn't been convicted for killing him."

"Are you trying to say DS Stuart didn't do his job properly?"

"I'm not saying that. I'm saying he's too close to it and angry his best mate is dead. He thinks I deserve everything I get."

The detective arched one eyebrow and wrote something on his pad. He placed his pen down and looked directly at me again. His piercing blue eyes made me feel uncomfortable.

"Anyway, yesterday I found out who was actually living next door in my old house."

"Go on."

"Kenny's two sisters. They threatened to make me pay for killing their little brother, in front of plenty of witnesses in court, and now they're living in my house – next door to where I'm staying."

"And you think these sisters are responsible for all the things you've mentioned today?"

"I'm fairly certain. It has to be. I mean, who else would want to punish me like this. And I'm terrified for Claudia too. Whoever shoved her down the stairs will want to finish the job, because when she wakes up she'll be able to name them."

"Understandable. Now, I'm sorry, but I'm going to have to get a colleague in as this is a little extraordinary. Would you mind going through it once more?"

I shook my head. "Of course not." I was just relieved that he seemed to be taking me seriously.

The detective left the room in search of his colleague.

"You guys can go, if you like," I said, conscious of keeping Rachel and her dad any longer.

"No way. We're going nowhere, are we, Dad?"

"If Margaret would prefer to be alone, then I think we need to do as she asks."

"That's not the reason. I'm very grateful you brought me, but the officer seems to believe me and Jake's not about, so there's really no reason for you to stay."

Mr Mendoza got to his feet. "Fair enough. How will you get home?"

"Dad!" Rachel squealed. "We can't just leave her."

"It's fine, Rach. Honest."

"No, it's not. You go, Dad. I'm staying to support my friend."

Mr Mendoza dug in his pocket and brought out a ten-pound note. "Here you go, then. I'll pay for the cab." And with that, he left.

"Tosser," Rachel muttered when the door had closed behind him.

"It's fine. At least he came. But did you see his face when he heard about what's been going on?"

A sudden smile lit up her face. "I thought he was gonna bust a blood vessel. He'll give me shit when I get home."

I nodded. "Only because he cares. You're lucky, you know?"

"I know, babe. I must seem like a total selfish bitch to you, but they're just so fucking stifling."

The door opened and the officer returned with a woman dressed in tight fitting, black trousers and a maroon blouse. She had coarse blonde hair and a ruddy complexion, but she had the kindest brown eyes I'd ever seen.

"This is Detective Inspector Ashley Kent," he said. "I've given her an outline of what you just told me, but maybe it would be best if you go through it again."

CHAPTER 35

"Intriguing," DI Kent said, when Maggie and her friend had left.

"So, what should we do?" Duncan asked, excitedly. As a junior detective, he wasn't used to getting any meaty cases.

"We?" She grinned.

"Aw, come on, boss. Give me a chance."

She gazed at him, a thoughtful expression on her face. "Okay, why not. But keep shtum and let me take the lead."

"Yes, boss. So what shall we do?"

"I don't know about you but I'm heading off home. We'll pay a visit to the sisters first thing in the morning,"

Deflated, he returned to his office. If she wasn't going to let him go around and arrest the Simms sisters tonight, he intended to do some research of his own – give himself some brownie points for the next day.

He read up on the death of Kenny Simms, and then he read the notes DS Stuart had entered into the system regarding the double murder of Matthew Pierson and Penelope Judd. On an impulse, he placed a call to DS Stuart's mobile.

"DS Stuart," a gruff sounding man said.

"Hi, Detective, I'm DC Jones from Central Manchester."

"What can I do for you, son?"

Duncan bristled. He didn't like the man's superior attitude. "I'm ringing about Maggie Simms."

"What about her?" now there was a cool tone to the older man's voice.

"I've just interviewed her regarding several allegations she's made against yourself and her stepfather's sisters."

"Allegations?"

"Yes. Could you tell me what your thoughts are? She thinks the Simms sisters are responsible for a number of deaths, including one of the cases you're working on, Matthew Pierson and Penelope Judd."

"Does she really? How interesting. What else did she tell you?"

Duncan paused, unsure of how much he should divulge.

"Spit it out, boy!"

"That you've got it in for her," Duncan blurted. "And that you want her locked up for the death of her stepfather, sir."

"Hang on a minute, *DC* Jones," he snapped. "Who is your superior officer?"

"Erm... DI Ashley Kent."

"And does Ashley know you're even contacting me? This is highly irregular."

"No, sir. I was acting on my own initiative."

"Take it from me, Sonny Jim, hang up now and don't mention this to Ashley or else you'll find yourself stuck on desk duty for the rest of your sorry career. Do you hear me?"

"I do, sir. Sorry, sir." Duncan hung up, fuming with himself. He still had a lot to learn and always seemed to be fucking up. He hoped DS Stuart wouldn't drop him in it with Ashley.

It was almost two hours later before Rachel and I hailed a cab. I was shattered.

"Shall I come back with you?" Rachel asked.

"No, honestly. Your dad'll have kittens if you don't go home after everything he heard tonight."

"Stuff Dad. He really pissed me off, leaving us like that."

"I'm glad he did. I felt his disapproval without even looking at him."

"Welcome to my world."

"You've got school tomorrow anyway. And I really don't intend to do much tonight."

"If you're sure?"

"I am."

The cab dropped me off first and I waved to Rachel as it drove away. I rummaged in my bag for the keys and glanced self-consciously at number eleven.

There didn't appear to be any lights on. I wondered if the sisters had already been arrested, but I doubted it. The detectives seemed keen to get some more information, but I didn't think they'd get around to actually questioning the sisters until DI Kent did her own research. She told me to keep out of their way in the meantime and she'd be in touch.

But keeping out of their way was easier said than done when we were living next door to each other.

I let myself in and filled the kettle. I'd not eaten all day and now I was starving. I warmed some leftovers from last night's dinner and carried a cup of tea and the plate of food through to the lounge.

A tap on the window startled me, making me spill my tea on the coffee table. "Bugger!" I emptied a wad of tissues out of the box and plonked it on top of the puddle before rushing to the door.

With the chain on, I peered through the small opening. I almost cried when I saw Jake on the doorstep.

"Good evening, Mags – oops, sorry – Maggie. Do you mind if I come in for a second?"

"What do you want? I'm just heading to bed."

"It won't take a sec, but I'd rather come in. You won't want every Tom, Dick and Harry to hear what I have to say." He nodded towards number eleven.

My heart dropped. I knew he'd been told about my visit to the station. I unfastened the chain and stepped backwards, allowing him to enter.

"Well, young Maggie. I've just had a very enlightening conversation with me old mate, Ashley. She told me you're no longer blaming me for bumping off all your allies and the pooch, but you now think it's poor Kenny's lovely sisters."

"Did you know they were living next door?"

"Of course I knew. Not much happens around here I don't know about."

"And yet you didn't think to warn me?"

He shook his head, and hitched his trousers up before taking a seat on the sofa. "Why would I have to warn you? They haven't done anything wrong."

"They blame me for killing their brother."

"The whole village blames you for killing Kenny. The fact is you *did* kill Kenny, didn't you?"

"Not like that and you know it."

"No. I know what you told everyone. Batting your eyelids and acting all innocent, but you don't fool me, Mags. Not for a second."

"What did you come over for, Jake?" I snapped.

"I'm the local detective. I wouldn't be doing my civic duty if I didn't check on you every now and then, considering you claim someone is out to get you."

"That's bullshit, and you know it. Listen, I get it. You were Kenny's best mate and you think I wasn't punished enough. But the fact is, he raped me. It wasn't just once either. He'd raped me repeatedly for months, since my mum became sick."

Jake belched out a laugh and slapped his thigh. "And yet

another change to your story. Oh my, you really do take the biscuit don't you, Mags?"

I knew it was pointless trying to make him understand. He hated me as much as I hated him. "For your information, I didn't need to go into it with Donna because she said it didn't matter when it began. She had enough evidence to prove it was self-defence."

"I've gotta give it to you, Mags. You've played a bloody blinder, getting everyone on side the way you have. But what makes you think your new neighbours hold any bad feeling towards you?"

I sighed and shook my head. "Why do you think, Jake? I killed their brother, for God's sake. Oh, and not forgetting the fact they threatened to make me pay when we were in court. I actually have lots of witnesses to that."

"Lots of people say things in the heat of the moment. It doesn't mean they intend to act on it."

"For a smart man you can be pretty dense."

He shot a flash of annoyance at me.

"You are. Why else would they have moved next door?"

"In their own words, they wanted to be close to their brother. His belongings are still inside, they never removed them. They lost touch with Kenny for one reason or another and they just want to lay their demons to rest."

"Believe what you want, Jake. Now, can you go, please? I need to go to bed."

"Is that a come on? Because I have no interest in you, Mags."

Horrified by his words, I felt my mouth gape open. It took a few seconds for me to respond. "How can you take that as a come on? You're as bad as your disgusting fucking mate. Now get out." I marched into the hall, and stood with the door wide open.

Jake strolled into the hall, stopping directly in front of me. "Be careful what accusations you throw around, Mags, because shit sticks. I might have no choice but to throw a few accusations in your direction."

I didn't react. I froze as he leaned in towards me, his rotten breath hitting my face.

Incapable of moving, I held my breath, body tight, as I silently screamed.

Jake leaned even closer to me, pressing me against the wall with his hard body, his face barely an inch from mine. "You'll beg me to fuck you sooner or later, Mags. Sluts like you always do." Then he licked my mouth and chin. The stench of tooth decay, stale fags, and coffee almost caused me to vomit in his face.

Terrified, I whimpered as he pressed his crotch into my stomach.

He eventually pulled away from me.

When I realised he was actually outside, I slammed the door behind him, shoving the bolts into place.

Relief flooded me. I pressed my back against the door as huge tears rushed down my cheeks, and I slid to the carpet. When was this nightmare going to end?

CHAPTER 36

At seven the following morning, Duncan and Ashley knocked on the front door of eleven Junction Road. They heard a commotion coming from inside. A woman, who appeared to be in her late forties, answered the door wearing a pale blue nightdress and matching slippers. Her puffy eyes were red rimmed from sleep and her frizzy brown hair stuck up above one ear.

"Miss Simms?" Ashley stepped forwards showing her ID.

"I'm Veronica Simms, yes."

"DI Kent and DC Jones. Do you mind if we come in for a second?"

"What for? Oh, don't tell me. Has the crazy cow next door called you?"

"Do you mind?" Ashley placed her hand on the door and the woman stepped backwards to allow them to enter.

She led them through to the kitchen. "Valerie, get down here!" she called up the stairs as they passed. "It's the police."

A series of thuds and thumps followed. Someone was stomping down the stairs.

A woman, who looked very like the first, only thinner, appeared in the doorway. "What's happened now?"

"Hi, Valerie. My name's DI Ashley Kent. I wonder if we can ask you both a few questions down at the station?"

"You've got to be joking. What on earth for?" Valerie said, both hands flying to her mass of mousy brown frizz.

"We'd rather do this at the station. Could you both get dressed for me, please?"

They weren't impressed. They shouted and swore and kicked up a fuss, making Duncan blush. He was relieved Ashley was taking the lead, as he suspected he wouldn't have been able to speak without stuttering, a condition he had suffered from as a child and sometimes still did, in stressful situations.

When at the station, they split the sisters up and left them to stew for half an hour while Duncan and Ashley had a coffee. When they finally returned to the first interview room, Veronica was seething.

"About bloody time. What the hell is this all about?"

"What do you think it's about, Veronica?" Ashley asked as they settled down opposite her.

"How do I bloody know? All I can think of is that silly murdering bitch next door."

"You mean Maggie, your niece?"

"She's no fucking niece of mine."

"What could she tell us that would make us bring you in for questioning?"

"Who knows? I've barely set eyes on her since we moved in. She went mad at Val the other day, though, and seemed surprised we were renting the place."

"Why *are* you renting the house your brother died in? If you don't mind me asking?"

She shrugged her meaty shoulders. "We wanted to be close to

him. He was our baby brother. It broke our hearts when we discovered that bitch had murdered him."

"When did you last see your brother?" Duncan asked.

She flushed deep red. "Fifteen years ago."

"Why so long?"

"He stopped talking to us when he moved to Manchester. We didn't even know where he lived at first – but then Val found him three years ago and we travelled from the Isle of Wight to meet up with him, certain he would be overjoyed at a reconciliation. But he blanked us. We were devastated."

"What reason did he give for not talking to you?" Ashley asked.

"Oh, something and nothing. You know what families are like – complex."

"Yeah, I know families. But it's pretty uncommon for siblings not to forgive one another anything." Ashley raised her eyebrows.

"Not Kenny. He was as stubborn as a mule – always had been since he was a boy."

"So, you decided to drop everything and move from the island to live in the house he lived and died in?" Duncan said.

"I'm not expecting you to understand, young man. Kenny meant the world to us, regardless of what he felt. We came up with the intention of collecting his belongings, but when we found out the house was up for rent we made the call to leave it all as it was."

"Like a kind of shrine?" Duncan asked.

"Call it what you like. I don't need to justify myself to a little pipsqueak like you. I've done nothing illegal."

Her words stung. It pissed him off when people mentioned his age. He was actually thirty, but still looked like a gawky teenager and his voice lacked the timbre an adult male usually developed at puberty.

Ashley placed her hand on his arm. She must've been able to sense his frustration and wanted to take the reins again.

"No, moving house isn't illegal, Veronica, but murder is," she said.

The older woman almost fell off her seat. "What the hell are you on about?"

"It must drive you mad knowing the girl who killed your precious brother is still walking the streets."

She shrugged. "So what if it does. She got away with it. The court failed him."

"So you decided to take it upon yourself to put that right, did you? Make her suffer the way you suffered?"

"No. Of course not."

"Where were you on the first of August?" Ashley asked.

"Still on the island. We didn't arrive here until last week."

"And can you prove that?"

"If I must. Both Valerie and I worked at the prison. They will be able to corroborate our story."

And what about the..." Ashley glanced at her notepad. "Fifteenth of August?"

"Same answer. Now are you going to tell me what it is you think I've done?"

Ashley ignored her question. "And you never came up to Manchester before that?"

Veronica rubbed her brow as though to ward off a headache. "Obviously we came up when we first heard about Kenny. But we didn't stick around, and then we got a train back up on the morning of the court date."

"Did you return the same day?" Duncan asked.

"Yes, we did."

"We'll need proof. Do you still have your train tickets?"

"I will do, somewhere, I'm sure."

Ashley glanced at Duncan, her eyebrows arched, before turning to Veronica. "Did you ever meet DI Donna Sullivan?"

"Yes. She was the detective in charge of Kenny's murder."

"What did you think of her? Do you think she did her

job well?"

"At the time, I thought she was taken in by the fake innocence of the girl?"

Ashley narrowed her gaze. "Why fake innocence?"

"It's obvious. Even Jake Stuart didn't believe her, but he said she gave a good performance that deserved an Oscar."

"Did he now?" Ashley said, her jaw clenching. "And what about the shopkeeper?"

"What fucking shopkeeper? Look, I'm starving and I need to get home. So either spit it out what I'm supposed to have done or just take me home, please."

"The local shopkeeper gave a pretty damning account of your brother and that swung it for the judge."

"So?"

"She was burned to death in her shop a week later."

"And you think it was me?"

Ashley arched her eyebrows. "Detective Donna Sullivan was also killed. And, lo and behold, so was Maggie's solicitor. See a pattern emerging?"

"This is outrageous. Should I be calling a solicitor?"

"That's up to you, but it will take a few hours no doubt, and we haven't charged you with anything yet."

"Did you ever meet Claudia Green?" Duncan asked.

"Never heard of her."

"Your next-door neighbour."

"Oh, the older woman. Yes, I met her once just after Kenny's death. She's a right battle axe."

"And since you moved here?"

"I haven't seen sight of her. Just the girl and her friend."

Ashley pushed her chair out noisily and got to her feet. "Okay, Veronica, we'll go and see what your sister has to say."

"But what about the old woman? Is she dead too?"

Ashley ignored her and walked from the room.

Duncan followed close behind.

"What do you think?" he asked Ashley in the corridor.

She scratched the back of her head. "I've a feeling she's telling the truth. We'll see what her sister has to say and then we'll need to get hold of the prison and see if they were both working on those dates. If so, we'll have no choice but to release them."

CHAPTER 37

I don't know how long I stayed on the mat behind the front door. It felt like everything that had happened over the last few months had come crashing down around me and I couldn't seem to shake it off.

I eventually crawled to the sofa where I spent the rest of the night.

By morning, I had calmed down enough to make a cup of tea. I called the hospital to see how Claudia was. I'd made it clear to all the nurses that I expected them to contact me at even the smallest change, but I still insisted on calling every day, and felt dejected every single time they told me she was just the same.

I sipped the tea. A blackness had descended on me – I couldn't seem to shift it. I pushed the cup away, feeling like I might throw up at any moment. Then I curled on the sofa again.

I thought about going back to London. Staying for Claudia when she wasn't even aware I was there wasn't working, and I was putting myself in danger after everything that had happened. The police had been supportive, but I knew how far-fetched my story sounded.

Although aware my phone was vibrating inside my bag, I

didn't have the energy to reach for it. I'd never felt so bad. Even losing my mum and the awful chain of events with Kenny hadn't made me feel as though I didn't want to talk to anybody, or even get dressed.

I knew I should be heading to the hospital. I hadn't been since Wednesday, and today was Friday. I knew Rachel intended to come to stay for the weekend and I desperately needed to go food shopping, but I really couldn't force myself to move. I brushed away tears with the back of my hand and closed my eyes to shut out the world.

I hated feeling like this, but I had no choice. I hoped it wouldn't be long before I came out the other end of it.

I slept the morning away and was woken mid-afternoon by someone hammering on the front door. My heart stopped. Was it Jake, back to finish what he'd started?

"Open the door, you cowardly bitch!" one of Kenny's sisters shouted through the letterbox.

I groaned and pressed a cushion over my head, trying to block out the hateful words. When I heard the door slam next door, I allowed myself to breathe again. And once more, the tears flowed.

I stayed on the sofa for the rest of the day, only leaving to go to the toilet, but I hurried back right after. I was a wreck and knew being like that wouldn't do me any favours.

I was startled again when I heard somebody knocking at the door.

"Maggie, are you there?" Rachel peered at me through the window.

It took all my strength to get to my feet and open the door.

"What the...?" Rachel said, rushing in and slamming the door behind her. "Are you okay, Maggie? Has something happened?"

I plonked down on the sofa and sighed. The words just wouldn't come. I didn't know what was wrong with me, so how could I possibly tell her?

"You're worrying me now, Maggie. Is it something to do with those nasty bitches next door?"

I shook my head. "No. Although they did come over earlier, screaming and shouting at me through the letterbox."

"You're joking? The cheeky mares. Did you call the police?"

I shook my head.

"Maggie! You should've called that detective – have they even arrested them yet?"

I closed my eyes, trying to block out the fifty thousand questions.

"Should I call them for you?"

"No," I snapped. "They must have questioned the sisters as they were ranting at me for something. But they clearly didn't charge them if they let them out so soon."

"I can't believe it! So all that last night was a waste of fucking time?"

I shrugged. "Seems so."

"Is that what's wrong with you? Are you scared they might try to attack you next?"

I shook my head. "I honestly don't know. Jake came around last night and he's such a dick. It's clear he's poo-pooed my side of the story which is no doubt why they didn't lock them up."

"What else did Jake say?"

I shrugged. "Oh, you know. He's a nasty prick – I don't know why I let him upset me, but he really scared me last night. I wish I hadn't let him in."

"I'm calling my dad. Jake needs to pull his fucking neck in."

"No, please, Rach. I'd rather just leave it. I've decided to go back to London next week if there's no change with Claudia. College has been hassling Agnes when I'll be back."

Rachel sat back down and rubbed at her temples. "I was talking to Mum this morning. She's agreed you can come to stay with us until Claudia wakes up."

"Really? What made her agree to that?"

"Dad told her what you told the cops and Mum freaked out. She doesn't want me to stay here while there's a nutter on the loose."

"You don't need to stay here, Rach. I don't want to put you in danger too."

"I couldn't stand leaving you alone last night, and by the sound of things, it seems I was right. I told Mum either I stay here with you or you come to stay with us, and she agreed."

"I dunno, Rach. I'd rather not. I know your parents aren't my biggest fans."

"I've told you, it's nothing to do with you, Maggie. It's only because they worry about me."

"I get that. But it's not nice to think you're an unwanted guest in somebody's house."

"You are wanted – by me. I want you to stay. The house is so big you won't even have to see much of them."

I sighed again. "I don't think so, Rach. I'd rather just go back to London. I'm tired of trying to cope with everything. I've realised I'm too young to be dealing with all this shit alone. And I don't have to. I raced here to support Claudia and care for Sandy and we all know how that turned out. At least in London, I'm looked after. All I have to deal with is my classmates' gossip and ridiculous amounts of homework. That's enough for me."

She didn't respond, but her eyes and mouth conveyed her disappointment.

"I'm sorry, Rach. We can stay in touch, but I really can't see another way."

"There is another option."

"Go on."

"My nan's house is still empty. We could both stay there for now."

"I'm sure your mum would be thrilled about that."

"She's been saying she's worried it will attract the local deadbeats while it's empty – at least this way it'll solve all our problems."

I thought about it for a second. "It could be a temporary solution if your mum agrees to it."

"She will, but I'll talk to her tomorrow if it makes you feel better."

I smiled and felt a lot brighter than I had all day.

"Now. What shall we have for dinner? I'm starved."

We decided to call out for pizza and, while we waited I told her everything Jake had said to me the night before. She was fuming, but I made her promise not to tell her dad. At least if her mum agreed to us staying at her grandmother's house, then I wouldn't be in any position for Jake to corner me again.

———

Valerie Simms had told Ashley and Duncan the same version of events as her sister had. A phone call to HMP Isle of Wight, their place of work at the time, confirmed they were working long shifts on the dates in question.

"What if they got one of the inmates to do the killings for them upon his release?" Duncan asked, desperate to solve the case by any means possible, and gain some kudos from his colleagues.

"That's a bit of a giant leap, Duncan." Ashley's eyes danced with mirth.

"Just a thought, boss. Someone's responsible. All those deaths can't be coincidence. I just wonder why Jake Stuart didn't make the connection."

"I have a feeling Jake Stuart had his own agenda. But don't worry, I dragged him over the coals this morning. I told him he either looks over each of these cases again and comes up with some kind of evidence to prove he's done his job or I'll take it to the DCI."

CHAPTER 38

"What time will you be back from the hospital?" Rachel asked over a breakfast of microwaved, leftover pizza.

"I haven't been for two days, so I feel I need to stay for a little while. You're going to see your parents anyway, aren't you?"

Rachel nodded, chewing and flapping her hand at the mouthful of hot pizza.

"If you take the back door key, at least you'll be able to let yourself in if you get back before me."

"Cool. If Mum's okay with it, when would you want to move to Nan's?"

"Probably tomorrow. I don't have much stuff to take but I'll need to speak to Doreen and ask her to keep an eye on the house and I'll also need to call Agnes and Fred."

"Sounds okay. Maybe you could speak to your college about transferring back here?"

I shook my head. "No. I don't think so, Rach. I can't think about staying here long term, and the thought of going back to school after everything that's happened was the reason I left in the first place."

"Yeah, but it's different now. We're friends again and I'll make sure nobody talks behind your back."

I still shook my head. "I don't think so."

"Just think about it. It would be cool if we were in college together – I really miss you."

"I know, and I feel the same, but too much has happened. I'm anonymous in London and that's how I like it."

We walked to the bus stop together before going our separate ways.

I found Claudia the same as I left her on Wednesday. It was disheartening that her condition didn't seem to be improving despite the assurances from the medical team. When I questioned them again, it was clear they didn't have a clue why she hadn't recovered from her fall.

Again, I spent the day reading to her and jabbering about everything and anything. As I was preparing to leave, the nurse told me they were taking Claudia for another scan to see if they could work out what was happening inside her head.

Rachel's phone buzzed as she entered Claudia's back yard. It was a message from Maggie telling her she would be later than she first thought.

A loud bang behind Rachel caused her feet to leave the concrete. Whirling round, she sighed with relief to see it was only the door to the old coal shed blowing open in a sudden gust of wind.

She let herself into the kitchen and made a coffee, miffed that Maggie wouldn't be back for ages. She couldn't wait to tell her the good news, that her parents had agreed to them staying at her nan's house for a while. She hoped Maggie would agree to stay, for now at least.

In the living room, she kicked off her shoes and got comfy in front of the TV.

A knock at the door a short time later caused the hair to stand up on her arms. *Who the hell's that?*

A peek through the lace curtain answered that question. Detective Jake Stuart peered back at her.

"Ah, Miss Mendoza," he said as Rachel opened the door. "I need a chat with Maggie. Is she there?"

"She's at the hospital visiting Claudia," Rachel said, her voice flat.

"Is she due back? I need to speak to her. It's important."

"Shouldn't be long. Have you arrested the neighbours?"

Jake shook his head. "I'm afraid I can't tell you anything. Do you mind if I come in and wait for Maggie?"

Feeling wary of him after what he'd done to Maggie, Rachel took a step backwards and reluctantly allowed him to enter. She didn't know whether or not to confront him, or to remain calm and try to get him onside. She chose the latter. "Can I get you a coffee?"

"I'd appreciate that, Rachel."

"It's instant, sorry."

He grinned. "Is there any other kind?"

She led him through to the kitchen. She figured it was probably the safest place to be if he intended to turn nasty.

"So," Jake continued, "as Maggie's closest friend, tell me what you think about the recent events."

"I told the cops at the station the other day someone is targeting her. It's true."

"Have you ever actually witnessed anything yourself, or is it just what Maggie's told you?"

"I was here with her when the dog turned up dead. We'd been outside to look for him and there was nothing there, but when we looked later on, his body had been left on the doorstep."

"And you didn't see or hear anybody?"

Rachel handed him a steaming mug of coffee. "We'd been cooking in here at the time, probably chattering and catching up, but we didn't hear a thing. I know what you're thinking, but Maggie is the victim in all of this."

"I'm beginning to think you're right."

Rachel frowned. "You do?"

"I admit, at first I thought she had an overactive imagination. But I've been looking into each of the cases as a whole rather than individually and something's come to light."

"Really? What?"

"I really need to speak to Maggie first. But I can tell you a car has been sighted approaching each scene."

"A car? Whose car?"

"I'm still looking into it. We're trying to locate the registered owner."

"So you think she's right. Someone *is* targeting her?"

He screwed his face up a little. "Its early days, and the sighting of the car could be a genuine coincidence."

"I'm just relieved you're taking Maggie seriously. It's terrifying to think she could be the next victim. Do you mind if I peel some potatoes while we talk?"

"Not at all."

Rachel found a colander in the cupboard and opened the bag of potatoes. She rummaged in the drawer for a knife. "My parents will be pleased if you find out who's responsible. They're worried *I* might be the next victim." She pulled on a pair of rubber washing-up gloves, and picked up her first potato.

"Understandable. I mean, you're here all alone. How easy would it be for somebody to get to you?"

She shuddered. "Don't say that. I've already had a scare today. It seems Maggie's paranoia may be catching."

"Why? What happened?"

"When I was in the backyard earlier, I almost died when the old coal shed door swung open and banged onto the wall behind me. I know it's normally locked and I thought someone might be inside."

"Mind if I take a look?"

"Erm." Rachel shrugged. "Okay."

She followed him out to the shed, barely breathing. The door still swung free.

He cautiously stepped inside, flashing his torch into the darkness. "Nah, doesn't look as though anybody has been in here in—" His words were halted as Rachel plunged the knife deep in the centre of his back.

CHAPTER 39

I waited until Claudia was brought back to the ward, but I needn't have bothered. The nurse told me we wouldn't get the results of the scan until the next day.

I messaged Rachel as I left the hospital.

Heading 2 bus stop, where r u?

> *Running late, should we*
> *meet at Lardoes, my treat?*

Gr8, c u there

I arrived at the café before Rachel and ordered a coffee while I waited. She arrived ten minutes later looking immaculate, as usual.

"Gosh, look at you all dressed up. I feel like a scruff. It's been a long day."

"I forgot to grab the back door key before we left this morning, so I stayed at Claudia's. And anyway, Mum's paranoid about me being there at all, never mind on my own."

"Yeah, I don't blame her – I didn't even think about that."

"But I have some exciting news. Mum said it's okay to move into Nan's for a while."

"Did she? And she doesn't mind?"

"She had a whinge of course, laid down the law: no boys, no parties, no mess."

I shrugged. "Understandable."

"Yeah, I expected much worse."

"Should we order? I don't think they'll be open very late." I indicated the waitress at the counter who seemed to be cleaning out the coffee machine.

We both ordered cheeseburger and chips. Rachel chose a bottle of juice instead of a coffee, considering the coffee machine had been partially disassembled.

"So," Rachel said as we returned to our seats. "I was wondering if you'd like to go to Nan's tonight?"

"Tonight? It's getting a bit late. Why don't we leave it until tomorrow?"

"Dad said the weather forecast isn't great for tomorrow. And we'll need to get a cab anyway, so why not tonight?"

"No reason why not. I'll need to make sure Claudia's house is tidy though."

"We'll have plenty of time to go back and blitz the cleaning ready for Claudia coming home."

"True." I nodded.

The waitress appeared with our food.

"We'd best eat up, then, if we're moving house tonight."

We laughed and I suddenly felt much lighter.

Back home, it took us little over an hour to pack my stuff and give the house a quick tidy. By nine thirty, we were sitting in a taxi for the ten-minute journey. It felt nice to leave the street. I doubted I'd ever return for anything more than a quick visit.

Rachel's nan's compact, two-bedroomed bungalow was immaculately decorated in cream and beige tones throughout. Rachel bagsied the master bedroom, but I didn't mind – it was her grandmother's home after all.

After I'd unpacked my things in the sparsely furnished bedroom, I fell into the armchair opposite Rachel in the lounge, and groaned.

"Knackered?" she asked.

"It's been a long day."

"You'll be able to sleep in tomorrow. Are you going to the hospital again?"

"I'll see how I feel. I really wanted to speak to the specialist about the results from her scan."

"Wouldn't they tell you over the phone? We could spend the day together instead. I'm back at school on Monday – couldn't you go to see Claudia then?"

"We'll see. I'll need to call the detective and tell her where I'm living. I honestly thought I'd have heard from them today, if only to tell me what happened when they questioned the sisters."

"I wouldn't call them. If they need to speak to you they have your number. What if it *is* Jake terrorizing you? Do you really want to tell him where to find you?"

"That's true. But what can I tell them if they want to come to meet up with me?"

"Just meet them at Claudia's. There's no reason to tell them you don't live there."

"Yeah, you're right."

The next morning, the ringing of my phone dragged me from a

deep sleep. I forced my eyes open and glanced at the clock. My stomach did somersaults. It was seven a.m. My first thoughts were of Claudia.

"Hello?" My voice sounded shaky to my own ears.

"Hi, Maggie, it's Detective Ashley Kent."

"Oh, hi? So it's not about Claudia?"

"Sorry?"

"No, it's okay. I was just shocked with it being so early – I thought it might be the hospital."

"Ah, I get you. No, it's nothing to do with Claudia. I'm actually calling about Detective Jake Stuart."

"What about him?"

"He came to visit you yesterday afternoon and he hasn't been seen since."

"Really? I haven't actually seen him for a couple of days."

"Are you not staying at Claudia's house?"

"Erm… Yeah, why do you ask?"

"Because I'm outside, knocking on the door and there doesn't appear to be anybody home."

"Oh, I stayed at my friend's last night."

"I need to speak to you. I'll come to you. What's the address?"

"I don't know. I'll come home. Give me twenty minutes and I'll be with you."

CHAPTER 40

I hung up and quickly dressed. Then I ran through to the other bedroom. 'Rach?"

"What the hell?" She rubbed her eyes groggily.

"I've had a call from that detective. She's at Claudia's and I said I'd go back there now."

"What time is it?"

"Seven. She said they're looking for Jake – apparently he's gone missing after going to visit me yesterday afternoon."

"I didn't know you'd seen him yesterday."

"That's the point – I didn't."

"What are they on about then?"

"I don't have a clue. Listen, I need to get back there. I'll see you later."

She jumped out of bed. "I'll come with you, hang on."

"I need to call a taxi anyway, so if you want to come, you'll need move it."

"I'll be right down."

As the taxi turned the corner, I gasped. Three different police cars were parked in the middle of the street outside Claudia's.

"What the hell?" Rachel said.

I shook my head. "Do you think they're here to arrest the sisters?"

"Who knows? But I'm sure we'll soon find out."

I paid the driver and approached the crowd of people on the pavement outside number eleven.

Detective Kent stepped forward when she spotted me. "Ah, Maggie. Thanks for coming back so soon. May we?" She indicated Claudia's front door.

"Oh, yes. Hang on." I scrambled around in my bag for the keys and led Detectives Kent and Jones, through to the living room.

"Right," Detective Kent said, when we were all seated. "So, since speaking to you earlier, we've actually discovered DS Stuart's car parked along the street."

"This street?"

She nodded.

I looked at Rachel, who seemed as confused as me.

"That's bizarre," I said. "He hasn't been around here since the other night."

"He left a message with a colleague to say he was on his way over here as he'd discovered something about your case and wanted to ask you a few questions. He obviously came over as his car is parked along the street, and your neighbours have confirmed it's been there overnight."

"I'm just as puzzled as you," I said.

"Do you have any objection to my team looking around the property?"

"Of course not."

She nodded at her colleague and he got to his feet and left the room. Moments later, several uniformed police entered the house, passing the living room door.

My stomach was doing somersaults. What could've happened to Jake? What had he discovered about the case?

A shout from the rear of the property made Detective Kent leap to her feet. "Wait here," she said, and raced from the room.

I grabbed Rachel's arm. "I have a bad feeling about this."

We had no idea what was going on, but whatever they'd found scared the crap out of me. It reminded me so much of the night Kenny had died. I wanted to curl into a corner and cry.

After what seemed like an eternity, Detective Kent returned. She appeared shocked and her face had drained of colour.

"I'll need you to accompany me to the station, Maggie."

"What's happened? What did you find?"

"I need to read you your rights. Margaret Simms, I'm arresting you for the murder of Detective Jake Stuart. Anything you say, can and will be taken down in evidence and used against you in a court of law."

I gasped. My mind reeling. I couldn't speak. I snatched a glance at Rachel, who had pulled her hands away from mine and was shaking her head.

"Do you understand, Maggie?" the detective asked.

I nodded. Blinking uncontrollably. I allowed myself to be led to the street and into the car, a familiar numbness descending on me. I didn't see what happened to Rachel and wondered if she was still sitting on the sofa, her mouth open. She wasn't used to shit like this. Not like me – this was the third time in a few weeks I'd been arrested for murder.

———

At the station, Detective Kent put me in a cell. She was apologetic which made me think she didn't really believe I was responsible for Jake's death.

I didn't even know where his body was found, but I presumed it was in the kitchen considering that was where the most activity had been. At least I now knew Jake wasn't the killer. Detective Kent told me he'd made a discovery of some sort, so maybe he finally believed me and confronted the sisters.

I couldn't feel sadness for his death. So what if he wasn't actually the killer, he *was* a nasty bully and he'd frightened me more than once. In fact, I was glad he was dead.

CHAPTER 41

The detectives returned a short while later. When they'd gone through all the formalities, they settled down on the opposite side of the table to me.

"Are you sure you wouldn't like me to call a solicitor?" Detective Kent asked.

I shook my head. "No. I'd rather just get this over with."

"Okay." She smiled warmly, and took a deep breath before continuing. "As you're no doubt aware, we found the body of Detective Jake Stuart at your home this morning. "

I nodded. "How did he die? Do you know?"

She flashed her colleague a glance. "I'd say it had something to do with the knife sticking out of his back."

My eyes widened at the news of yet another knife attack. "And you think I did it?"

Detective Kent shrugged. "It's no secret that you and Jake didn't get on."

"Maybe not. But that doesn't mean I'd kill him."

She shrugged again.

"I haven't seen Jake since Thursday night when he came around to threaten me."

Another glance passed between the detectives.

"Threaten you? What about?" Kent asked.

"Just his whole vibe was threatening. He said he didn't believe my story and almost said I deserve everything I get for killing Kenny. He tried to make out I was coming on to him because I asked him to leave so I could go to bed."

"Did he touch you?"

I shook my head. "I thought he was going to, but he didn't. He just licked my face."

"Jake did?" she asked, clearly shocked.

I nodded. "It was disgusting."

Yet another glance passed between the two detectives.

"So, where were you yesterday?" Detective Jones spoke for the first time.

"I went to the hospital in the morning and stayed there until late."

"And you can prove that, can you?" he said, his tone a little off.

"I'm sure the nurses can vouch for me, but there was a staff change during the day."

Detective Kent cleared her throat and glared at her colleague, before turning back to me. "When did you return to the house?"

"I met Rachel for dinner and we went back together to pick up some of my things. I stayed with her last night."

"So you didn't go back to the house alone at any stage?"

"No. Rachel stayed with me on Friday night, we left together yesterday morning and we returned together last night."

"We've checked the knife used on Jake. It's part of a matching set in your kitchen drawer."

"How did he even get inside?"

"Who?"

"Jake? Wasn't he in the kitchen?"

"He was in the outhouse."

"Oh."

"Then how did somebody get inside to steal a knife? Nobody else had a key."

"So you're still saying you had nothing to do with it?"

"Of course, I am. I didn't see Jake. Check with the hospital if you don't believe me. What time did he go missing?"

"The last contact anybody had with him was at three p.m. He was on his way over to see you."

"And what had he discovered?"

"He didn't say. He wanted to check something out first."

"So, Jake finally found some evidence, but nobody knows what it was?"

"How do we know it was evidence to support your claims? It could've just as easily been that he found something to dispute them or, better still, put you in the frame," Detective Jones sneered.

Detective Kent put her hand on his arm as though to say, back off.

"So, I'm fucked. Is that what you're telling me? Jake may have been killed because he found some evidence against the killer, but it wasn't me. Whoever has been trying to frame me has done well, hasn't he? "

"He?" Detective Kent cocked her head to one side.

"Or her. I don't know, but my money's on the sisters. Did you even question them?"

"Yes, we did. They have watertight alibis for all the dates in question."

"Convenient, don't you think?"

"Not at all. They hadn't even moved to the area until well after Claudia had her fall."

"Really?" That stumped me. I had no clue who else it could be.

"'fraid so," she said. "So I'm sure you can see the dilemma we have. All these deaths and accidents surround you. Anybody who you've blamed in the past is either dead or was nowhere near here at the time."

"That's stupid. I was in London when Claudia fell."

"Claudia's accident could very well be just that, an accident."

"So what you're saying is, I killed Donna, Yazz and her husband, Matt and his girlfriend, Sandy, and now Jake?"

"Unless you can think of anybody else who had issues with all these people?"

"You know I can't. But you guys didn't think the first few deaths were suspicious until I brought them to your attention."

"Classic behaviour," Detective Jones said.

"What are you on about?"

"It's common knowledge that serial killers crave recognition for their crimes."

"Oh, for God's sake. So I'm a serial killer now?"

He shrugged. "You tell me."

"I've been *telling* you all along. This whole thing began when I killed Kenny in self-defence. Somebody clearly wants me to suffer for it otherwise they'd just get it out of the way and kill me instead. They probably even want me to do time for murder. It's clear they think I got away with it in the first place."

"But who else is left, Maggie?" he said. "You've got nobody else to blame."

"The sisters."

Detective Kent pushed her chair away noisily. "We're wasting time going over this. We'll be back soon." She looked at her colleague and tipped her head towards the door, and then they left.

"You're one lucky young lady," Detective Kent said when she returned around an hour later.

I looked up at her questioningly.

"The hospital have confirmed you were there all day until late."

"Does that mean I can go home?"

"Yes. I'm just waiting for the CCTV footage showing what time you left the hospital to match that with the time you met up with Rachel at the café."

"There may be a discrepancy as I arrived a while before Rachel."

"Don't worry. We already have an officer interviewing the café staff."

"Thank God for that. So, if you believe my story, that means there's a killer out there. Have you any other leads?"

"Not yet, but it's early days. Needless to say, Maggie, you're still our chief suspect, so don't leave the area without clearing it with us first."

By two p.m. I was on the bus heading back to the village. I dialled Rachel's phone as soon as I sat down.

"Maggie! Oh, my god. I didn't expect to hear from you for ages," she squealed. "Dad's been calling the station, but they wouldn't tell us a thing."

"Where are you now?"

"At home – Mum and Dad's. How about you?"

"On the bus heading to your nan's. Claudia's house is still a crime scene and I won't be allowed back there yet."

"Do you even want to go back? I don't think I could face it, knowing Jake… you know."

"I wasn't sure if your parents would have changed their minds about me staying at your nan's."

"Course not. I'll get Dad to drop me there now. See you soon."

CHAPTER 42

Rachel was already at the house by the time I arrived. Thankfully her dad hadn't hung around – I didn't have the energy to go through any further interrogations today.

Rachel ran down the path and hugged me like a mother welcoming her long lost child. *"Oh my god!* I honestly didn't think I'd be seeing you for a while!"

"Imagine how I felt." I grimaced.

We walked inside, arm in arm. "So how come they let you go? Do they believe you?"

"They didn't at first. Thank fuck the CCTV at the hospital confirmed my story. But I'm still not off the hook. Jake was killed with one of Claudia's knives."

"You're joking! I saw he was outside, so I guessed the sisters must've got to him."

"That's what I thought, but they have alibis for all the other murders – they didn't come back to the area until after Claudia's fall and Matt's murder, and they can prove it, apparently."

"So who…?" She shook her head.

I shrugged. "I've no idea."

"You would tell me, wouldn't you?"

"Tell you what?"

"You know I wouldn't blame you, don't you?" Rachel said.

"What? Do you think I did it?"

"I didn't say that. I just wondered… He's been harassing you for weeks."

"Rachel!"

"What? I'm only asking."

I was stunned. "I'm going for a lie down, if that's okay with you."

"Maggie! Don't be like that."

"Like what, Rach? You mean, don't be offended that my best friend thinks I'm a cold blooded killer?"

"That's not what I said, and you know it."

"Whatever!" I stomped off to my little bedroom and closed the door. I climbed onto the bed and hugged the pillow to my chest. I felt utterly miserable.

I missed my mum. I'd blocked out the feelings for months now, and I guess I blamed her in a way. My life had turned to shit when she'd been diagnosed with cancer. But she'd taken an essential part of me when she died and I realised I hadn't even mourned her, not really. The time I should have been coming to terms with my loss was instead taken up with Kenny and my fight for survival.

I cried for what felt like hours, but eventually fell asleep. I woke to semi darkness and noticed a congealed cup of tea on the bedside table. I guessed Rachel must've left it there.

I felt ashamed for going off at her earlier. She was the only person I had left in the world who actually cared about me, and the last thing I wanted to do was turn her against me too.

I slid from the bed and padded through to the lounge. Rachel was lying on the sofa watching TV. "Hey, Rach."

She sat up and patted the seat beside her.

I settled next to her and tried a smile.

"Friends?" she said.

"Friends." I nodded. "I'm sorry for being so touchy, but for the record, I didn't kill Jake. Although, I won't deny that the real killer did me a huge favour."

"I'm sorry for asking you like that. And of course I didn't really believe you could've been responsible."

"I know you didn't."

"Are you okay? I heard you crying and I really didn't know whether or not to come in."

"Yeah, I'm fine. It was just the last straw, you know? I miss my mum so much. When she first died, I was relieved as I'd hated seeing her in so much pain. But then the time I should have used to mourn her was instead taken up with Kenny raping me and then self-preservation."

"Your mum would have been devastated to see everything that's happened to you. You were her world."

I nodded. "I know that. But can I tell you a secret?"

Her forehead furrowed. "What?"

"That night with Kenny wasn't the first time."

"You mean...?" Her face paled.

"He'd been forcing me to have sex with him the whole time Mum was sick."

"No! He couldn't have been. You said it was just the once."

"I didn't tell everyone the truth at the time because I didn't want anybody thinking bad of my mum."

"Why would they?"

"Because, that last night, he told me Mum knew all about it."

Rachel jumped to her feet and walked to the window, her back to me.

"I don't know if he was lying – I hope so, but I don't know."

"Your mum wouldn't have allowed that, Maggie. She'd have defended you to the death."

"In my heart, I know you're right. But my head keeps replaying his words over and over."

"If he'd been doing it for weeks, why was that last night any different?"

"Because he made it clear he didn't plan to leave me alone. He wanted to live as a couple."

Rachel shook her head. "I'm sorry. This is just too much to take in. Can we talk again tomorrow? I think I need an early night."

Confused, I watched Rachel walk away and heard her bedroom door close. What had upset her so much? Maybe I was wrong to confide in her after all.

CHAPTER 43

I sat staring at the muted TV screen for a while, trying to process what had just happened with Rachel and to make sense of the situation. My stomach growled and I realised I hadn't had anything to eat all day. Detective Kent had offered me a sandwich, but I couldn't face food at the time. I headed through to the kitchen and scoured the empty fridge. I was relieved to find a can of minestrone soup in the back of one of the cupboards and I warmed it in the microwave.

I worried about Rachel. She'd been so supportive of me up to that point. Maybe it was because I'd kept the truth from her all this time?

I took Rachel's place on the sofa and watched mind-numbing TV. At eleven, I made my way to bed and was startled by the ringing of my phone on the bedside table.

"Hello?" I whispered.

"Maggie?"

"Yes."

"It's Sister Robinson from The Manchester Royal. I'm phoning to let you know that Claudia's finally awake."

I was stunned. "I'll be right there." I hung up and rushed to Rachel's room.

"Rach!" I called, popping my head inside her door.

I was surprised to see her on her laptop.

"What's happened?"

"Claudia's awake. I'm going to the hospital now."

"I'll take you."

I paused. "What in? Your flying machine?"

"No, silly. I have Nan's little car in the garage. It's automatic and real easy to drive. She used to give me lessons in it."

"I didn't even know you could drive, but I do know you don't have a licence."

"Where's your sense of adventure? There'll be no bus for ages, and a taxi will cost you a fortune."

She was right. I hadn't thought about how I was actually going to get there. "But I'd feel terrible if you were stopped by the police."

"I won't get stopped. I've been driving it all over for weeks and nobody's noticed, not even you."

I laughed. "I think I'd have noticed if you were driving, Rach."

"I had the car parked along your street the other day and doubled back when you got on the bus."

"Why? Why be so secretive?"

"Because I know how much you worry and I didn't want to give you cause to – you've got enough on your mind."

"Then why now?"

She shrugged. "Needs must. Now are you coming or not?"

She grabbed a set of keys from a hook by the back door and led me through an internal door I'd thought was just a cupboard, into the small windowless garage that housed a small gold-coloured car.

"Mum was planning on selling it, but I convinced her to keep it for when I get my licence. She'd have kittens if she knew I was already using it."

I shook my head. "But I still don't get why you are. Your dad runs you around all over the place and you're usually such a wuss when it comes to breaking rules." I climbed into the passenger seat, still unsure but desperate to get to the hospital whichever way possible.

She hit a button on the sun visor and the garage door sprang to life. When she started the engine and turned on the lights, it suddenly struck me that we were actually doing this.

"Are you *sure* you can drive?"

"Who's the wuss now? Trust me. I know what I'm doing."

She pulled out of the garage and drove the car surprisingly well all the way to the hospital. My heart was in my mouth as we approached the city, but she didn't flinch even when we passed two police cars at the side of the road.

We found a car park right outside the front of the hospital and security buzzed us in the front door.

I recognised the nurse on the main desk. She recognised me and grinned. "Great news, hey?"

"Is she still awake?"

She chuckled. "Yes. Go and see for yourself."

"Shall I wait here?" Rachel said.

I glanced at the nurse. "Maybe just go alone for now. She's still pretty drowsy, so we don't want to over stimulate her."

I nodded. "I won't be long." I squeezed Rachel's arm.

"Take all the time you need."

The light in Claudia's room was dimmer than the corridor and the curtain was partially pulled.

I cautiously walked further into the room, brimming with excitement yet terrified at the same time. When I first saw her, my stomach dropped. She looked no different.

I approached the bed and placed my hand on hers.

Her eyes slowly opened and she smiled.

"Oh, Maggie." Tears filled her lovely, smiley blue eyes.

"Hey, you. How are you feeling?"

"Oh, you know. A bit shit."

I barked out a laugh. "I'm sure you do. But I'm so pleased you're awake. I've been so worried."

"Have you?"

"Yes. I've been here almost every day since it happened."

She appeared confused. "How long?"

"A few weeks. But let's not worry about that, for now."

"Weeks?" She shook her head and closed her eyes for a second. "Sandy?"

My heart stopped. How could I tell her about her darling dog. "I've been staying at your house. I've got so much to tell you, but I'd rather wait until you're feeling better in a day or two."

She patted my hand. "You're a good girl, Maggie." She closed her eyes again.

"I'll leave you to rest, and come back tomorrow. I just wanted to see you were okay."

She could barely muster the energy to nod, and smile at me.

I bent and kissed her cheek before leaving.

Rachel was sitting in the day room reading a magazine. She jumped to her feet when I appeared in the doorway. "What's wrong?"

"Nothing. She's tired so I said I'll come back tomorrow."

Rachel looked relieved. "Did she say what happened to her?"

"No, and I didn't ask. She's still a bit out of it. She did ask about Sandy though."

"Shit. What did you say?"

"I avoided it. There's no way I could just blurt it out like that."

She nodded. "It's going to be hard on her regardless of when you choose to tell her."

"I know that. But I was thinking I may not tell her anything. It's best if she thinks he just ran away."

"She'll find out eventually though."

"Yeah, but at least it can wait until she's up and about again."

"I guess so."

"Let's get home. I'll come again in the morning and maybe she'll be more with it."

CHAPTER 44

The next morning I called Detective Kent and told her about Claudia. She said she'd come in to see if she was up to being questioned later on that day.

I declined Rachel's offer of a lift to the hospital, choosing instead to catch the bus. It was less hassle, and far more legal. She left for school in the car.

I wondered how much longer she'd have kept the fact she was driving from me if I hadn't been living at her nan's. I didn't really want any part of it. When her parents found out, and I had no doubt they would, I didn't want to be blamed.

I picked up a couple of newspapers and women's magazines from the newsagents on the ground floor of the hospital. I was sure Claudia would want to catch up with what had been going on in the world.

Claudia was sitting up and appeared much brighter than she had last night.

"Ah, there you are, duck. I've been dying for you to come back and tell me all I've been missing."

I took a deep breath and sat in the chair beside her. "I brought you something to read. I figured you'd be itching to know what you've been missing."

"I didn't mean with celebrities, silly. I meant with you."

"Gosh! Maybe I should wait to get the all clear from the doctor? There's so much to tell you, but I'd hate to make you ill again."

"Sod the doctor. I want to know."

I chuckled, thrilled to see her fall hadn't altered her personality. "Okay. I think the police will be in to speak to you this afternoon, so I guess you'll find out everything anyway."

"You're worrying me now. What's happened?"

"Can you remember the night you had your fall?"

"It's hazy. The last thing I remember was going to bed and Sandy wouldn't settle. I thought he needed to go wee, so I ended up getting up again and heading for the stairs. I don't remember anything else until I woke up in this bed last night. I feel there might be more, dancing around on the edge of my subconscious like when you can vaguely remember a dream but not the details. Does that make sense?"

I nodded. "I honestly wish you could remember. You see, the thing is, I'm sure you were pushed."

Claudia's eyes widened. "Pushed? By who?"

I shrugged. "I've no idea. We were hoping you could shed some light on that. But whoever it was left you for dead."

"Who found me?"

"Doreen found you. Matt let me know and I came right away."

"Thanks. I'm sorry to interrupt your school work though."

"Ah, don't worry about that. I'll catch up."

"So, what else. I know there's more."

My eyes filled as I tried to find the words. "Matt and his girlfriend were killed."

Claudia gasped and her hand flew to her chest, which had turned a deep blotchy red.

I dabbed at my eyes with my sleeve.

"Don't tell me there's more."

I nodded. "I'm sorry, Claudia. Sandy ran off one night. When we found him a while later…" Tears rolled freely down my face. "He was dead too."

She buried her head into her pillow and the sound of her sobbing broke my heart.

"Why? I don't understand why anyone would hurt my poor baby."

I stroked her arm, feeling helpless. "I think he may have seen the killer and they didn't want him identifying them."

"Them?"

I shrugged. "Kenny's sisters have moved into number eleven. I was certain it must be them, but apparently they weren't in the area until long after Matt's death. I was hoping you'd remember."

She shook her head. "I can't remember a thing. I wish I could. I'd string the bastards up with my bare hands for hurting my poor Sandy."

"There's more."

Claudia groaned.

"Another person I'd suspected was Jake Stuart. He kept coming around, taunting me. But, during our slanging match, we both agreed the deaths of Detective Sullivan and Yazz and her husband were also connected. I thought it was him, and he accused me."

"But you no longer think that?"

"Nope. Jake was killed in your old coal shed the day before yesterday. One of your knives was used and the police arrested me, but CCTV showed them I was here all day."

"How did they get one of my knives?"

I shook my head. "Don't know. Does anybody else have a key to your house?"

"No. Oh, hang about, Doreen may have one?"

"Did you ever give one to my mum?"

Claudia closed her eyes as though deep in thought then opened them again. "You know, I do remember giving her one when I went into hospital for a procedure a few years ago, but I can't remember if she gave it back or not."

"I'm wondering if Kenny's sisters could have found it. My money's still on them – who else could it possibly be?"

Claudia closed her eyes again for a moment as though trying to remove the mental images.

"I'm sorry. I honestly didn't want to tell you like this."

"I needed to know," she said, as though breathless. "Tell me, what did you do with poor Sandy?"

"He was taken away and cremated. I thought we could do something special to remember him when you're feeling better, maybe scatter his ashes at the park."

Claudia placed a trembling hand on my arm. "I'd like that, duck."

I grasped her fingers with my other hand. "In the meantime, we need to focus on getting you back on your feet. I'm ecstatic you're with us again. I truly thought the longer it went on, the less chance we would have of you waking up."

"I'm back now. And I don't intend going anywhere again for a good while."

"Thank God for that."

"Detectives Kent and Jones said they will be in later to talk to you. Do you know how long you'll have to stay here for?"

Claudia shook her head, her eyes clearly heavy – it had been a tough morning.

"You have a nap. I'll just be here, reading your magazines." I grinned at her as she seemed to fall asleep mid-smile.

As promised, the detectives arrived just after two. They were clearly disappointed when Claudia told them she couldn't remember a thing.

Although still weak, she told them off for treating me like a criminal.

Jones bristled. His top lip curling slightly and I could tell he wanted to bite back, but DI Kent put her hand on his arm and smiled sweetly at Claudia. "We're just doing our job, Mrs Green," she said, before backing out of the door.

I followed them into the corridor. "Any idea when we'll be allowed to return to the house?"

"Is she…?" DI Kent pointed towards Claudia's room.

"I'm not sure when she can go home, but I need to clean her house before she does."

"I'll double check with the team, but I'm sure we should be finished there tomorrow at the latest."

I watched them leave and then I walked into the day room to call Rachel.

"How is she?" Rachel asked as soon as she picked up.

"Tons better than she was, but still exhausted."

"What did Mulder and Scully say?"

"Who?"

"The cops – don't you watch the X-files?"

"Never heard of them." I chuckled.

"Oh, well, maybe they're not cops after all. It's a stupid programme my mum watches."

I shook my head. "I should be leaving here around five. Are you home yet?"

"I didn't go in today. Couldn't face it, after everything."

"Your mum'll have a fit when she finds out."

"She'll be fine. Mondays are always slow anyway."

"Because that's the day most people wag it."

"I'm hardly wagging it." She laughed. "Shall I pick you up? We could go shopping right after."

"I don't want to get in the car with you, Rach. You're not even insured."

"Suit yourself. I'll meet you at the supermarket at five thirty, if you like."

I could tell by her snotty attitude that she wasn't happy with me. But I couldn't just sit back and say nothing. She'd be in big trouble if she got caught.

"Great, see you then."

CHAPTER 45

Claudia was struggling to sit up when I returned.

"Ah, Maggie. Shove this pillow behind my back. That's a good girl."

I helped her get comfy and then sat down beside her on the armchair.

"So what did they say?" she asked.

"Who?"

Claudia rolled her eyes. "Who do you think?"

"Oh, nothing. I was just asking them if they'd finished at the house so I can go back and make sure it's all nice and tidy for you."

"You're a good girl." She patted my hand. "I can't wait to get in my own bed, I can tell you." She then frowned. "If the police are still all over my house, where are you staying?"

"I've stayed at Rachel's nan's house the past couple of nights."

"Oh, friends with *her* again, are you?"

"I am. And she's been great, Claudia – a true friend."

She pulled a face.

"What's that for?"

"True friends don't dump you in your hour of need."

I nodded. "She's apologised for that. She just didn't know how to be around me. I understand and I've accepted her apology."

Claudia didn't need to say another word; her tight-lipped expression spoke volumes.

"I know how it looks, and I was a bit wary at first, but she'd made a mistake. I honestly believe her."

Claudia shrugged. "What about the stuff she told Matt? He said if he was to use her as a witness you'd be locked up by now."

That stumped me. "What do you mean? What did she say?"

"He didn't go into detail, but she indicated you were getting a name for yourself around school."

"Name? What kind of name?"

Claudia looked down at her hands and picked at her fingernails.

"Tell me. I have a right to know."

She took a deep breath before lifting her head to look directly into my eyes. "She said you were sleeping your way through the school."

My breath caught in my throat. I jumped to my feet and went to the window.

"I'm sorry. I really didn't want to tell you like this."

Turning to face her, I placed my elbows on the back of the armchair. "I don't get it. Why would she say such a thing?"

"I don't know. But we didn't believe her. In fact, I'd say she's the one who sleeps around."

"No, you're wrong. She doesn't even have a boyfriend."

"Maybe because boyfriends are beneath her."

I shook my head. "What's that supposed to mean?"

"She's into older men."

I laughed. "Rachel? Rachel Mendoza?"

Claudia raised her eyebrows in confirmation.

"Who?"

"I've said enough already. Why don't you ask her yourself

because you won't believe me until you hear it from the horse's mouth?"

Her words were swimming around in my head without making any sense. Firstly, why would Rachel tell Matt I was sleeping around? And who was the older man she was seeing? And how come I was only just hearing about all this now?

I glanced at my watch – almost 4.30. I'd arranged to meet Rachel at the supermarket in an hour, so I guessed I'd be getting some answers then.

Claudia dozed off again while I pretended to read a true life story from one of her magazines. At just before five, I kissed her cheek and left to catch the bus.

Could Rachel have been seeing Matt? The way Claudia said it, it was clearly someone we both knew. But there didn't seem to be any sign of a boyfriend anymore, which is why I thought Matt could've been the one. But if that was the case, why hadn't Rachel told me? I couldn't figure this out and I was desperate to talk to Rachel.

I arrived at the local Asda with five minutes to spare and went to the toilet. Rachel was standing beside the trollies when I came out.

"Oh, you're here," she said. "I was just about to call you."

"I needed a wee." I grabbed a trolley and we entered the supermarket. I wanted to blurt it out, ask her, but how could I? The store was crammed full of shoppers.

"How's Claudia?" she asked, piling two loaves in the trolley.

"She's good, yeah," I said, tight-lipped.

Rachel glanced at me and squinted. "You okay?"

I nodded. "Just tired."

After collecting a few items, we headed to the checkout, splitting the bill in half. I found myself sneaking the odd glance at her, questioning if she could have really said those things to Matt. If I just blurted it out, there was a chance I could lose her friendship again.

We each carried two bags and headed to the exit.

Rachel turned towards the steps to the underground car park.

"Don't tell me, you brought the car anyway."

She shrugged. "I'm not going to walk all the way home with this lot when I can drive."

I sighed. I'd really wanted to talk to her on the walk home. "I'll let you take the bags, but I'm not getting in the car, Rach. I've been in enough trouble to last me a lifetime."

"Suit yourself." She wrinkled her nose haughtily. "What's wrong with you anyway?"

"Nothing."

We reached the bottom of the steps.

"Maggie..."

"Okay. Have you been seeing someone?"

Her eyebrows furrowed as she pointed in the direction of the car. "Me?"

I nodded.

"Seeing someone?"

I nodded again.

"No. Why?"

"It's just something Claudia said."

"What else did she say?"

We reached the car and Rachel placed the bags on the ground while she searched for her key.

"Nothing."

"Come on, Maggie. I know you."

I took a deep breath. "She said you told Matt I was sleeping around."

She picked up the bags and put them in the boot. I placed mine beside them. "You've got to be having a laugh."

I shook my head as my phone rang. I didn't recognise the number so I answered it.

"Maggie?" a male voice said.

"Yes."

"It's Detective Jones. Can you talk for a minute?"

"Yeah. What about?"

"I wanted to let you know we've found what Detective Stuart was working on before he died."

"Really? What was it?"

"It seems, after examining the CCTV, there was a small gold-coloured Toyota seen approaching each of the crime scenes."

My world crashed to a stop. I struggled to breathe yet I knew I had to maintain a calm appearance. I tried to stay upright on jelly legs and my heartbeat thudded in my ears, deafening me. I casually glanced towards Rachel who was standing a couple of feet away from me. "Really?" I said, trying to keep my tone level.

"We've traced the last registered owner, but it seems it belongs to an elderly woman who's currently in a nursing home. What I wanted to know is, have you seen any cars matching this description hanging around at all?"

I chewed my lip and smiled at Rachel. "Er, no. Sorry."

"Never mind. It was worth a shot. We hope to interview the woman tomorrow, but we don't hold out much hope of getting any information. The nursing home staff said she's got dementia."

"I see. Oh well, good luck." I was struggling to keep the tremor from my voice.

I ended the call and turned to Rachel. "Okay, you get going and I'll see you back at the house."

"Who was that?"

I looked at my phone, stalling for time. "That? Erm, that young detective we met the other day. I think he fancies me."

She squinted, clearly not buying it. Then she shut the boot and walked to the driver's side. "Get in, Maggie. It's only around the corner."

"I'm not getting in the car, Rach. I'll see you there." I set off at a brisk walk, giving her no chance to argue.

When outside, I crossed the road and headed down a side street before pulling my phone from my pocket again. My fingers trembled so much I struggled to ring the detective back. I almost cried as he answered the phone.

"Yes, Maggie?"

The words wouldn't come, and I was aware I was panting into the phone.

"Maggie? Are you okay?"

"I... I know who it is. The killer, I know who it is."

"Okay. Go on."

Startled by a screech of tyres, I spun around to see Rachel speeding towards me. I could see her face clearly through the windscreen and knew she planned to kill me.

I screamed and dropped the phone. "Rachel, no!" My body had frozen. There was nothing I could do to prevent the car slamming into me.

My feet left the pavement and I crashed into the brick wall of the terraced house beside me. A white hot explosion went off in my head. I faded out.

I was vaguely aware of being lifted, but I couldn't force myself to open my eyes. An excruciating pain in my leg caused me to scream in agony. Rachel was dragging me along the ground.

I couldn't bear the pain as a blackness descended on me.

CHAPTER 46

"Shit, boss," Duncan Jones said as he rushed into DI Kent's office. "I think I just heard Maggie getting attacked."

"What the...?" Ashley jumped to her feet and grabbed her jacket from the hook beside the door.

He quickly told her what had happened.

"Casey," she said to her assistant, "I need you to track Maggie Simms' mobile, and send me the co-ordinates."

Casey nodded and tapped furiously on the keyboard.

"Let's go."

The two detectives ran to the car and Ashley got in the driver's seat.

"So, tell me once more. Where did she say she was?"

"She didn't. She said she'd been shopping and was on her way home. When I first spoke to her, she seemed vague, as though somebody was listening. Then she called me back a couple of minutes later and she was in a panic. She said she knew who the killer was, but she didn't get a chance to tell me. The next thing I knew, she screamed and I heard the phone clatter to the ground."

"What else did she say?"

"Nothing. Oh, hang on, she did say something. *No, Rachel.*"

"Rachel?"

He nodded.

"Are you sure?"

"I heard it loud and clear."

The car phone rang.

"What've you got for me, Casey?"

"The phone is at nineteen Abbottsford Lane."

"Great, Casey. Now, see what you can find out about Maggie's friend, Rachel. Her details are in the file."

"Will do, boss." The line went dead.

"Do you really think that pretty young thing could be responsible for all the deaths?" Duncan said.

Ashley gave him a sidelong glance. "You were only too eager to blame Maggie and she's the same size."

"True. But Maggie seems much tougher somehow."

"Only because she's had to be. Rachel, on the other hand, has been indulged her whole life. Her father's a real toffee-nosed snob."

"I didn't realise you knew him."

"We met him the night Maggie came in to make her statement."

Duncan doinged the heel of his hand off his forehead. "Oh, yeah. I forgot."

They pulled into Abbotsford Lane. Number nineteen was the middle of the row. Too-short grey net curtains hung at the manky window.

They climbed from the car and Duncan tapped on the scuffed yellow front door.

They heard somebody bouncing down the stairs before the door swung inwards.

"Who the fuck are you?" The woman wore a grimy white T-shirt and little else.

"We're looking for Margaret Simms. Is she here?" They both held up their ID.

"Never heard of her." The woman went to slam the door, but Duncan put his foot in the way.

"If she's not here, then how come her phone is inside your house?"

The woman opened and closed her mouth like a trap. She shook her head. "I didn't steal it. I found it lying on the pavement."

"Go get it. Now!" he said.

She scurried off and appeared moments later with the white iPhone.

Duncan took it from her. "Tell me what you saw."

The woman scowled. "Fuck off! I'm not a grass."

"Either you tell us what you saw, right now. Or I'll drag your skanky arse down the nick and throw the book at you."

"All right, all right, take a chill pill, man. I didn't see much. The girl with the phone was hit by a car, that's when she dropped it."

"Then what happened?"

"The driver dragged the girl over to the car and lifted her into the boot."

"Tell me what the car looked like?"

"It was gold. I don't know the make."

"One last thing – what did the driver look like?"

"Another girl. One of them rich-bitch types, you know with glossy long hair, and a snotty face."

Ashley and Duncan ran back to the car. Ashley called through to Casey again as Ashley sped from the street.

"I was just about to call you, boss," Casey said. "I didn't find much on Rachel Mendoza, but when I checked out her parents, I realised her mother's maiden name is the same as the owner of the gold car."

"Yeah, we've just worked that out, too." Ashley said. "Text me the old woman's address, and alert the Armed Response Team – we may need their assistance. I don't want to take any chances. This girl has killed enough people already."

CHAPTER 47

My head pounded and from the agonizing pain in my leg, I knew I'd broken it. I couldn't make out where I was at first – it was dark – but, from the movement, I figured I was in the tiny boot of the car.

My heart raced. The stifling air surrounding me was hot, and sweat broke out over my whole body. "Rachel," I wheezed, the breath stuttered within my chest. I checked my jacket pocket for my inhaler. Nothing.

"Rach?" I said louder not sure if she could hear me but tried to keep my tone lighter, hoping to be able to talk some sense into my suddenly deranged friend. "Rach, let me out! Can't we talk about this?"

"What is there to talk about?" Her voice was muffled but I could hear her. "I was willing to leave it alone, but that wasn't good enough for you, was it?"

"I don't know what you mean. Please, Rach. I think my leg is broken – I need to go to the hospital."

"Oh, you know all right. Questioning me, pretending you and I were still mates. I'm not a fucking idiot!" She yelled the last bit and it was clear she was past the point of reasoning.

She turned a corner causing me to shoot backwards and smash my already throbbing head on the car.

It took a few minutes for me to clear my thoughts enough to try again. "Rachel, please. Listen to me. We are still mates, I swear. I didn't believe a word Claudia said to me."

She didn't respond, but I could hear her sobbing.

"Rach. Speak to me, please. Tell me what's wrong and how we can put it right. You're my best friend."

"That's bullcrap, and you know it. I saw you with that other girl. The goth. Acting all giggly, like best mates, as though you hadn't a care in the world."

That threw me. "She's just a mate. I promise you, Rach." I hadn't picked up on her jealousy of Caroline. I couldn't even remember them being in the same place for more than five minutes. "Is that what all this is about? My friendship with Caroline?"

"You stupid bitch. It's not all about you, you know."

The car came to an abrupt stop and I rolled backwards, screaming with the pain in my leg. I bit my lip and tentatively turned myself, resting my leg in the least painful position. I could hear Rachel ranting to herself, and what sounded like her banging her hands on the steering wheel. Grateful we were no longer moving, I took several deep breaths before trying to reach out to her once more.

"What's it all about, then, Rach? Tell me. You know you can tell me anything."

She mumbled something again, but I couldn't make out the words above the steady thrum of the engine.

"I can't hear you, Rach. Let me out so we can talk."

"What's the point? It's all over now, anyway. I heard what that cop said."

"I don't know what you're talking about. Please. Let me out."

"The car! Fucking Jake left a trail and it will lead them straight to me."

My worst fears were suddenly confirmed. "Are you saying...?"

"Come on, spit it out. Are you asking me if I tried to shut him up? Course I did, you stupid bitch."

I was suddenly aware the boot was filling with fumes. "Rachel. What's that smell? Let me out. I'm begging you."

"If only you'd told me the truth sooner. He said he loved me. That we would be together."

I tried not to inhale deeply, but I was beginning to feel sick. What was she on about? Was Jake the boyfriend? "I don't get you. Were you seeing Jake?"

She laughed. "You are one stupid bitch, do you know that?"

"Then tell me. Who are you talking about?"

"We were planning to be together. That's what he told me. Said he'd wait for me to leave school and we would marry, but until then, I had to keep our affair secret."

I still couldn't work out who she was talking about. But I could tell her speech was becoming slurred too. "Who was it? And what does it have to do with me?"

"When she became... sick I was glad. It would mean we could finally be together."

The realisation slammed into me. "Kenny? You were sleeping with Kenny?"

"Of course... it was Kenny. We were together for... three years. I can't believe you never... noticed."

I gasped.

She began to cough.

"Rachel? There's a leak of some kind. It's making us sick. Please, let me out."

Silence.

Feeling woozy, I closed my eyes and let myself sink down into the darkness.

CHAPTER 48

Duncan jumped from the car outside number twenty-one, leaving Ashley to park up. He approached the front window of the bungalow and peered through the glass shading his eyes. The lounge was empty.

He crept around the house, doing the same with each window, but there was no sign of anybody.

A steady humming sound confused him, but he couldn't work out where it was coming from. He cocked his head to the side and held his breath, trying hard to make it out. He jumped out of his skin as Ashley rounded the corner in front of him.

"Anything?" she whispered.

"No. Nothing."

"Let's go for a drive. They can't be far."

Back in the car, Ashley put another call through to Casey.

"There's no sign of anybody at the house. Find Rachel's mobile number and track it."

"On it."

"Also, can you run the number plate through the ANPR database? We need to find them, and fast."

"I have done, boss, but nothing's come up since yesterday."

"Which means they must still be local otherwise if they'd headed onto the main roads it would have been flagged."

"I'll check Mendoza's number, and get back to you."

They had made their way back to the supermarket when the phone rang a few minutes later.

"Did you get it?" Ashley barked.

"Yeah, it's showing the mobile is at the Findlay Street address."

"But we've just been there and there's no sign of anybody."

"Maybe she left her phone behind?"

Ashley nodded. "Shit! And there's been no sighting still?"

"Not a thing."

Duncan slapped the heel of his hand on his forehead. "They're in the garage. Quick, get back there."

"Did you hear that, Casey? Get me some back up at Findlay Street ASAP. You'd better make it an ambulance too." Ashley said, as she did a highly illegal three point turn and earned herself a chorus of car horn blasts from passing motorists. "Why didn't you check the bloody garage?" She shot him a fiery glance.

"There were no windows. I heard a strange sound and I was just about to investigate when you appeared around the corner and scared me shitless."

"So it's my fault you didn't do a proper job?"

Duncan exhaled from his nose like an angry bull. "I didn't say that, boss. I was distracted, that's all."

"Let's hope for your sake you haven't cost that poor girl her life.

As they pulled onto Findlay Street, they heard the sound of approaching sirens. Two marked cars skidded to a stop in the middle of the street seconds later.

Duncan didn't hang about. He raced to the garage door and tried to yank it upwards, but it wouldn't budge. The sound he had heard earlier was suddenly much louder and confirmed his suspicions. The engine was running inside.

He had first-hand knowledge of this kind of thing as his cousin had committed suicide in the same way. Contrary to popular belief, a hose wasn't needed for death to occur pretty damn quickly. He dreaded what awaited them on the other side of the roller door.

The uniformed police smashed through the front door and stepped aside to allow him and Ashley to enter first. As the male, he felt he needed to take the lead, although it was the last thing he wanted to do.

Half a dozen strides had him in front of the internal door. He braced himself, and covered his mouth and nose with his forearm before entering.

In the garage, he acted on impulse. He pounded the door opener with the heel of his palm and raced to the car to turn off the engine.

Rachel Mendoza was slumped in the driver's seat as though she'd closed her eyes for a nap. Ashley dropped to her knees beside her while Duncan rushed to the boot.

Another siren sounded in the street and, taking a glance, he saw an ambulance pull up and two paramedics jump out. He felt relief flood him, although he didn't hold out much hope by the looks of the first girl.

He opened the boot, and gasped at the sight of Maggie's unconscious and twisted body.

The paramedics were beside him in an instant, and pushed him out of the way.

He looked around to see Ashley. She was standing to the side of the garage and she had huge tears rolling down her cheeks.

She shook her head. "We were too late. We were just too late."

EPILOGUE

Claudia applied the finishing touches to her make-up. She hated funerals, and still didn't really feel strong enough, but she'd made a promise she would attend, and she never broke a promise.

She took a final glance at her reflection in the full-length mirror before heading downstairs. It seemed strange to be back in her own home. She still couldn't remember what had happened the night she fell, but the police were certain Rachel had been behind it.

She couldn't believe Maggie's best friend could've been responsible for all those deaths. She'd never trusted her, and Doreen had let it slip about the affair with Kenny. But an affair was one thing, murder was quite another.

DI Kent called around to inform her about the discovery they'd made on Rachel's phone. There were apparently hundreds of texts and voicemail messages from Kenny telling her how, when he was *free,* they would be together properly. He'd been grooming her for years.

It appeared Rachel had targeted everyone for supporting Maggie and, in her words, allowing her to get away with murder.

Rachel had even composed poems about each of the attacks. She hadn't believed Kenny had raped Maggie. She thought it had all been a collaboration of lies to help Maggie get away with killing him, which is why she turned on everybody.

Claudia stood in front of the mantelpiece. "Guard the house while I'm gone, little fella." She kissed the tips of her fingers and placed them on the pewter urn. She wasn't ready to sprinkle Sandy's ashes yet, but she intended to, one of these days.

She heard someone on the stairs.

"I'm in here, duck."

The lounge door flew open and Maggie clomped in, bashing her plastered leg with each step. In front of the mirror, she began pinning her hair up. "I don't think I can do this, Claudia."

"What? Your hair? Give it here."

Maggie batted the older woman's hand away. "No, not my hair. The funeral. I can't face it."

"We don't have to speak to anyone. We can just sneak into the chapel and sit at the back."

"Mr and Mrs Mendoza hated me before all this, and they probably still blame me for everything. No, I'm serious. I really can't face it."

"Then, if you're sure, we'll do something else instead. Any ideas?"

Maggie shrugged. "Could we go up to Werneth Low? My mum loved it up there."

"I think that's a wonderful idea. Your mum was my best friend. I loved her like a daughter, you know."

Maggie nodded. "She loved you too."

"Have you booked your train ticket for London?"

"Not yet. I'll do it later. Are you sure you'll be okay?"

"I'll be more than okay, duck. And I'll have your school holidays to look forward to. I have a feeling things are going to turn out just fine."

The End

ACKNOWLEDGMENTS

As always, I need to mention Paul, my long suffering husband. Your support means the world to me.

To my wonderful critique partners Susan, Marco, Jay, Sandra & Serena—you're the best.

To Mel, Ross, and all my friends and fellow authors—thanks so much for letting me bend your ear.

The wonderful ARC group – you're awesome.

To all the team at Junction Publishing - you are amazing!

And finally. To my wonderful family, especially Joshua, David, AJ, and Marley, my lovely grandsons, who give me immense joy. I am truly blessed.

ABOUT THE AUTHOR

My name's Netta Newbound. I write thrillers in many different styles — some grittier than others. The Cold Case Files have a slightly lighter tone. I also write a series set in London, which features one of my favourite characters, Detective Adam Stanley. My standalone books, The Watcher, Maggie, My Sister's Daughter and An Impossible Dilemma, are not for the faint hearted, and it seems you either love them or hate them—I'd love to know what you think.

If you would like to be informed when my new books are released, visit my website: www.nettanewbound.com and sign up for the newsletter.

This is a PRIVATE list and I promise you I will only send emails when a new book is released or a book goes on sale.

If you would like to get in touch, you can contact me via Facebook or Twitter. I'd love to hear from you and try to respond to everyone.

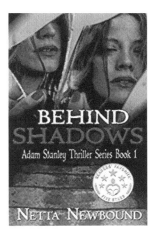

Amanda Flynn's life is falling apart. Her spineless cheating husband has taken her beloved children. Her paedophile father, who went to prison vowing revenge, has been abruptly released. And now someone in the shadows is watching her every move.

When one by one her father and his cohorts turn up dead, Amanda finds herself at the centre of several murder investigations—with no alibi and a diagnosis of Multiple Personality Disorder. Abandoned, scared and fighting to clear her name as more and more damning evidence comes to light, Amanda begins to doubt her own sanity.

Could she really be a brutal killer?

A gripping psychological thriller not to be missed...

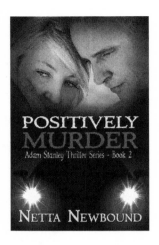

An Edge of your Seat Psychological Thriller Novel

For Melissa May, happily married to Gavin for the best part of thirty years, life couldn't get much better. Her world is ripped apart when she discovers Gavin is HIV positive. The shock of his duplicity and irresponsible behaviour re-awakens a psychiatric condition Melissa has battled since childhood. Fuelled by rage and a heightened sense of right and wrong, Melissa takes matters into her own hands.

Homicide detective Adam Stanley is investigating what appear to be several random murders. When evidence comes to light, linking the victims, the case seems cut and dried and an arrest is made. However, despite all the damning evidence, including a detailed confession, Adam is certain the killer is still out there. Now all he has to do is prove it.

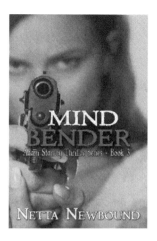

An Edge of your Seat Psychological Thriller Novel

Detective Inspector Adam Stanley returns to face his most challenging case yet. Someone is randomly killing ordinary Pinevale citizens. Each time DI Stanley gets close to the killer, the killer turns up dead—the next victim in someone's crazy game.

Meanwhile, his girlfriend's brother, Andrew, currently on remand for murder, escapes and kidnaps his own 11-year-old daughter. However, tragedy strikes, leaving the girl in grave danger.

Suffering a potentially fatal blow himself, how can DI Stanley possibly save anyone?

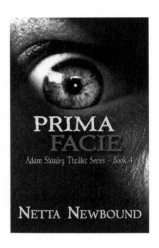

A Compelling Psychological Thriller Novel.

In this fast-moving suspense novel, Detective Adam Stanley searches for Miles Muldoon, a hardworking, career-minded businessman, and Pinevale's latest serial killer.

Evidence puts Muldoon at each scene giving the police a prima facie case against him.

But as the body count rises, and their suspect begins taunting them, this seemingly simple case develops into something far more personal when Muldoon turns his attention to Adam and his family.

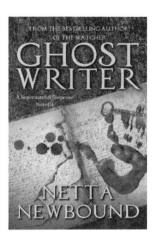

Ghost Writer is a 24,000 word novella.

Bestselling thriller author Natalie Cooper has a crippling case of writer's block. With her deadline looming, she finds the only way she can write is by ditching her laptop and reverting back to pen and paper. But the story which flows from the pen is not just another work of fiction.

Unbeknown to her, a gang of powerful and deadly criminals will stop at nothing to prevent the book being written.

Will Natalie manage to finish the story and expose the truth before it's too late? Or could the only final chapter she faces be her own?

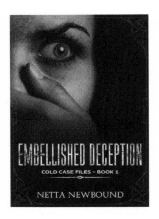

A Gripping and Incredibly Moving Psychological Suspense Novel

When Geraldine MacIntyre's marriage falls apart, she returns to her childhood home expecting her mother to welcome her with open arms. Instead, she finds all is not as it should be with her parents.

James Dunn, a successful private investigator and crime writer, is also back in his hometown, to help solve a recent spate of vicious rapes. He is thrilled to discover his ex-classmate, and love of his life, Geraldine, is back, minus the hubby, and sets out to get the girl. However, he isn't the only interested bachelor in the quaint, country village. Has he left it too late?

Embellished Deception is a thrilling, heart-wrenching and thought provoking story of love, loss and deceit.

An Edge of your Seat Psychological Thriller Novel

Geraldine and baby Grace arrive in Nottingham to begin their new life with author James Dunn.

Lee Barnes, James' best friend and neighbour, is awaiting the imminent release of his wife, Lydia, who has served six years for infanticide. But he's not as prepared as he thought. In a last ditch effort to make things as perfect as possible his already troubled life takes a nose dive.

Geraldine and James combine their wits to investigate several historical, unsolved murders for James' latest book. James is impressed by her keen eye and instincts. However, because of her inability to keep her mouth shut, Geri, once again, finds herself the target of a crazed and vengeful killer.

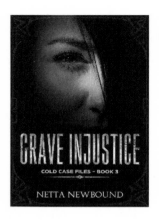

A Gripping Psychological Suspense Novel.

Geri and James return in their most explosive adventure to date.

When next door neighbour, Lydia, gives birth to her second healthy baby boy, James and Geri pray their friend can finally be happy and at peace. But, little do they know Lydia's troubles are far from over.

Meanwhile, Geri is researching several historic, unsolved murders for James' new book. She discovers one of the prime suspects now resides in Spring Pines Retirement Village, the scene of not one, but two recent killings.

Although the police reject the theory, Geri is convinced the cold case they're researching is linked to the recent murders. But how? Will she regret delving so deeply into the past?

THE BEST-SELLING SERIAL KILLER THRILLER THAT EVERYONE IS TALKING ABOUT

Life couldn't get much better for Hannah. She accepts her dream job in Manchester, and easily makes friends with her new neighbours.

When she becomes romantically involved with her boss, she can't believe her luck. But things are about to take a grisly turn.

As her colleagues and neighbours are killed off one by one, Hannah's idyllic life starts to fall apart. But when her mother becomes the next victim, the connection to Hannah is all too real.

Who is watching her every move?

Will the police discover the real killer in time?

Hannah is about to learn that appearances can be deceptive.

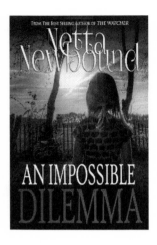

Netta Newbound

AN IMPOSSIBLE
DILEMMA

Victoria and Jonathan Lyons seem to have everything—a perfect marriage, a beautiful daughter, Emily, and a successful business. Until they discover Emily, aged five, has a rare and fatal illness.

Medical trials show that a temporary fix would be to transplant a hormone from a living donor. However in the trials the donors die within twenty four hours. Victoria and Jonathan are forced to accept that their daughter is going to die.

In an unfortunate twist of fate Jonathan is suddenly killed in a farming accident and Victoria turns to her sick father-in-law, Frank, for help. Then a series of events present Victoria and Frank with a situation that, although illegal, could save Emily.

Will they take their one chance and should they?

An Edge of your Seat Psychological Thriller Novella

All her life twenty-two-year-old Ruby Fitzroy's annoyingly over
protective mother has believed the worst will befall one of her two
daughters. Sick and tired of living in fear, Ruby arranges a date without
her mother's knowledge.

On first impressions, charming and sensitive Cody Strong seems perfect.
When they visit his home overlooking the Welsh coast, she meets his
delightful father Steve and brother Kyle. But it isn't long before she
discovers all is not as it seems.

After a shocking turn of events, Ruby's world is blown apart. Terrified
and desperate, she prepares to face her darkest hour yet.

Will she ever escape this nightmare?

Made in the USA
Middletown, DE
15 May 2023